A Whisper
of Angels

A Whisper of Angels

Lourdes R. Florido

LUMINOUS LIBROS

Published by Luminous Libros, Fort Lauderdale, Florida
booksoftherealm.com

Edited and designed by Girl Friday Productions
www.girlfridayproductions.com

Cover design: Emily Weigel
Project management: Devon Fredericksen
Image credits: cover © Jovana Milanko/Stocksy United; Sergey Lukankin/Stocksy United; donatas1205/Shutterstock; Trust Me I Drink Mint/Shutterstock; Bokeh Blur Background/Shutterstock

ISBN (paperback): 978-1-7358182-0-7
ISBN (ebook): 978-1-7358182-1-4

Library of Congress Control Number: 2020918851

*For Kyle and Tara—may you always find
an angel in times of darkness.*

PART I

Aground in the Beginning

CHAPTER 1

I sat on a bench in the square across from the wharf and stared at the *Ernestine* and her three rows of white sails ascending upwards like outstretched wings. I hoped her beauty and my art would help mute my rage, but I wasn't sure it would be enough.

It was dusk, and everything was quieting down, the merchants locking up their shops to head home while groups of mariners headed towards the nearby tavern. The *Ernestine* was the latest of the whalers to arrive in the harbor, having returned just a few days earlier, and I wanted to add her to my collection of drawings of all the ships that sailed in and out of New Bedford, Massachusetts. I wouldn't have much time to get a preliminary sketch before the shadows of the night took hold, and I didn't want to be at the wharf so long that I would have to deal with the people who populated the area at night. Already, as I hastily worked on my drawing, a loud, rather slurred voice interrupted me.

"Hey, I know him all to pieces."

A rotund, mud-splattered sailor swaggered towards me, followed by a tall one. *Oh hell, not now,* I thought. A couple of drunks was the last thing I needed.

"Nat, Nat, now stop; don't bother that boy," said the taller one. "We ain't here for the likes of him."

They were probably out looking for one of the wharfside prostitutes, who scurried out like roaches once darkness came. The mariners made New Bedford a more raucous place than someone of my quiet disposition liked, and 1857 had been a particularly loud and hectic year for our town. This month alone, a few dozen ships had gone out on the hunt for the sperm oil that made New Bedford one of the richest towns in America. The oil that came from sperm whales lit lamps and lubricated machinery, and our town was filled with all the makings of that industry, from immigrant sailors and wharf-side prostitutes to rich shipping agents and owners. We "lit the world" with our trade.

As I watched the two sailors stagger away, my thoughts returned to the source of my rage, recalling how my day had unfolded.

"Get out of that rack and get the hell out here, boy!"

I'd shuddered awake this morning to George Herrington's deep, booming voice, which roused me from what had been a peaceful dream of my father. In the dream, we were together again, on a sailing ship, staring out onto a purplish-tinged sea. For a moment my dream had felt so real, and I had been happy again—until reality in the form of Herrington's yells scared me awake and back to my misery. Before I could even sit up, he was in my room, shoving me off my bed.

"Did I not tell you last night to unpack my tools and set them in the sheds? Why are they still in the front sitting room?"

"It was too dark out there, and I thought it could wait until today," I said.

"Well your breakfast will wait then, until you're done unpacking those boxes," he snarled. "Get out there and do it now."

Bastard. Damn bastard, I thought, as I hurried out the back door, dragging one of his heavy boxes. I hated him. I could not wait until his ship left port for a hunt again—until First Mate Herrington went away for a long, long time. I still could not believe my mother had married him, and not even two months after Father was laid in the ground. What did she see in him? He was uncouth, and so young. It wasn't proper.

I had barely dragged the box into one of the sheds when he was bellowing again. "Hurry up and get to the other boxes, boy. Stop your dawdling."

The work and the endless browbeating continued for most of the day, until I could stand it no longer and just stopped. After dinner, when Herrington sat relaxing on the settee that Father had paid for, I finally let my face express just what I thought of him.

"Do not look at me that way, boy," he said.

"In what way?" I chided. Herrington jumped up, lunging for me, but I stepped back, right into Mother, who had come into the room.

"Nicolas, come here," she said, grabbing me by the shoulders and guiding me into the kitchen. "You cannot continue to treat George with disrespect," she said. "He is your father now."

"Never," I said. "*That* will never be my father. Mother, what were you thinking? He's so much younger than you; he's in his twenties! The thought of you with him sickens me."

She looked away for a moment and then quietly answered. "We need to move on with our lives, Nicolas. This is in everyone's best interest."

"But Father is barely buried," I blurted out. "You dishonor him, and you dishonor yourself. Do you know what the neighbors think? I overheard Mrs. Dorsett and Mrs. Barnes talking, and I was so embarrassed. Do you know what type of woman they are saying you are?"

She slapped me then, which surprised me, as she had never hit me before.

"I'm sor—" Mother began.

I didn't stay to hear what else she had to say. I ran to my room, grabbed my pencils and sketchbook, and ran out the back door to the wharf to draw.

And that is where I was now, attempting to continue my drawing. But my art would have to wait for another day.

"What? Up to this foolishness again?"

Before I could react to the voice that startled me, my sketchbook was snatched out of my lap.

"Idiot," I snapped, looking up to see Henry's smirking face, a prankish twinkle in his deep hazel eyes. He was dressed quite formally, in a dark blue suit, gold vest, and cravat. "Why so fancy?" I asked.

"I see you're wasting your time in this foul part of town again," Henry said, ignoring my question. "It's not bad," he said, assessing the drawing and dropping the sketchbook back into my lap. "But I have better plans for tonight."

"What?" I asked, knowing that whatever it was would probably involve some mischief.

Henry and I had been unlikely best friends since childhood, when we first met at the wharfside. We were different in so many ways. I was artistic; he, athletic. He was outgoing; I, introverted. And then there was the matter of our families. Henry's father was a wealthy whaling agent and ship owner, and Henry's family lived in a grand house on the hill and was visited by all the important people in town. My father, Sam, had been a blacksmith, and we lived in a small house near the wharf district. The only time we saw town "royalty"—other than Henry—was when they came to order something from my father. Yet, although we were very different, Henry and I had somehow connected right away. He once told me I wasn't what he had expected. I think he thought I would be like the sailors—rough and loud. A product of my class. "You are surprisingly refined," he told me.

But Henry was wrong to judge everyone to be the same. Although my father was a blacksmith, he was a quiet, reflective, and religious man who had never cursed in front of me, and although he was a tradesman, he was quite literate. I had been raised in a home where books were valued, especially the Bible, which he read aloud to me every Sunday.

And there was something else that connected Henry and me, a common interest that kept our friendship going. It was a love of trickery. I may have been quiet, but I loved pulling the wool over others' eyes. Through the years, Henry and I had played many jokes on schoolmates and others, like "haunting" the Roderick manor when they were away for the summer in Europe, which started so many rumors that the family feared to move back into their home when they returned.

"What are you thinking?" I asked.

"You will pretend to be me tonight."

"Why?"

"It's Father. He's met some new person, a Mr. Witham, who recently moved into town. He's a wealthy judge with a daughter around our age, and he and Father got to talking and arranged for me to have supper with the Withams and their daughter, Shelley, tonight. I do not want to sit through some God-awful meal with people who mean nothing to me, and this could make it interesting."

"Perhaps it won't be so bad," I said. "Maybe you'll find her pretty."

"You know I don't care," Henry said.

"Well your parents do," I said.

Henry's parents had decided it was time that he began thinking of a serious courtship. After all, by the time his father was our age—fifteen—he had already decided that Henry's mother would eventually become his wife. It's not like Henry couldn't have his pick of the girls in town. His family was rich, and he was handsome, his dark hair and eyes luminous against his fair skin. Girls blushed and giggled or flirted when they were near him, vying for his attention, but he never seemed to pay them much attention.

"Come on. Help me out here," Henry said.

"Okay." I mulled on it. "It could be fun, but I don't think it'll work. We don't look anything alike."

Our differences, like day and night, extended to our looks. I had inherited my father's fair looks, with light blue eyes and blond hair.

"Mr. Witham hasn't seen me yet," Henry said.

"Fine," I said, "but what about our clothes? These *chore* rags won't make anyone believe I'm the son of Mr. Lawton."

"We'll switch out of them. Let's duck behind the trees here."

"Okay," I said, watching Henry as he began tugging at his cravat and removing his coat. As we walked towards the clump of trees that bordered the back of the square, we suddenly heard the clomping of horses racing down the road. I looked up to see Henry's family's coach pull up to the curb. Inside was Mr. Lawton, and he did not look pleased.

"Just what are you doing, Henry?" he yelled, his displeasure with his son evident in his voice. "Oh, hello, Nicolas," he said, noticing me. "Henry, you are expected at the Withams, and Peters here told me that you asked him to drop you off at Nicolas's house instead. Frankly, I am quite surprised to see you both in this part of town at this time of night. Just what are you two up to?"

I didn't know what to say, so I remained silent, as did Henry.

"Well, we will talk about it later," Mr. Lawton said irritably. "Now get in the coach, dress yourself up, and I will take you to the Withams."

Henry sighed and glanced over at me, then followed his father's directions. As the coach rode off, I decided it was much too dark for me to continue drawing, so I headed home.

CHAPTER 2

Father was gone.

I still couldn't believe I would never see him again. Never at work in his sheds. Never at the dinner table. Never urging me to hurry up and go to the well. Never. Never. Never again. I stood in one of my father's work sheds, staring down at the black anvil where he had perfected his life's craft. Next to the anvil was a pair of horseshoes he had been working on. I picked one up and rubbed it, hoping to somehow feel close to him—to feel his essence. But there was nothing. As I mulled over my loss, I heard the back porch door at the house swing open and looked up to see Henry walking towards me.

"Nicolas," he called. "Are you in there?"

"Yes," I muttered.

"How are you holding up?" he asked, walking in.

"I don't know," was all I could muster.

"Let's get you out of here," he said. "I've told your mother that you're dining with my family this evening. Plus, I want to tell you all about my meal with the Withams last night."

"Fine," I said, letting him guide me out of Father's shed and away from my home. About thirty minutes later we were walking up the long red-cobbled stone path to Henry's house.

Even now, after all the times I'd been here, I was still intrigued by the structure Henry called home. It was one of the largest in town, a three-story gray building with a multi-gabled roof. The first time I visited, I remember thinking I'd get lost. There were so many spaces to explore, including a formal dining room, a parlor, a library, and a children's playroom, but my favorite room was a secret room accessible only from the library—its entrance hidden by a pair of sliding bookshelves.

In the room were a desk, some shelves with assorted knick-knacks from the Lawtons' travels, and an old sea chest, which Henry and I had gone digging through together. It held artifacts like the small wooden whale carving from Henry's father's younger days at sea. The chest also held his father's gun, which Henry's father had warned us not to touch, but we did anyway.

For Henry and me, the secret room was our fun room. We spent hours there playing chess and cards, talking about our lives, and planning the jokes we would play on others. We thought of the room as ours, a place where Henry could escape from his three little sisters and his own father's demands. I loved nothing better than spending a lazy summer afternoon there. But unfortunately, the darkness that had enveloped my life since my father's death made this visit less enjoyable. For the first time, I shared my feelings about my new "father" with Henry.

"Herrington is undeniably an ass," he said.

"Yes, and he's making my life unbearable. I don't know how much longer I can tolerate it."

"Well, you must do something."

"Yes, but what?"

"I say we give George a bit of our own brand of treatment, like we've done in the past to those who've bothered us. Like a combination of the Roderick haunting and the Linton scaring. Let's give George something to be afraid of, since he's nothing but a bully himself. But we need to plan this one out carefully. Let me think about it. In the meantime, I have some news to tell you. I'm attending my first formal ball next month. Shelley is also going to attend, and I think Mother and Father expect that she will soon be the girl of my dreams, or if not, that I will meet another socially appropriate girl who might be the one. The thing is, Nic, I, well, I just don't . . ."

He stopped.

"Just, what?" I asked, wondering what he was trying to tell me.

"It's . . . nothing, nothing," he said, suddenly looking somber.

"Did you like her?" I asked. "Was she pretty?"

"I suppose she is lovely," Henry said dispassionately. "She's blond and fair, like you. And she seems sweet, but I don't . . ."

"You don't what?" I asked.

"Well, let's just make plans for our haunting," Henry answered, ignoring my question.

And so we did.

CHAPTER 3

It took two weeks for our plans to come to fruition. We were pretending to haunt my father's work sheds. I knew it was wrong, pretending to be my poor father's ghost, but the thought that we could torment Herrington—enough to make him leave, or at least make his life miserable—overrode any common sense I had. So we put our plan into effect.

On the first night of our haunting, I dressed in Father's old work outfit—his apron, shirt, and pants—lit a few low candles to create a shadow, and at the stroke of midnight used the chisels and hammers in his shop to create a pounding ruckus. After a few minutes, I looked through the window and saw Herrington and my mother peering out of their bedroom window in astonishment at my shadow at work with the tools. When I saw Herrington back away from the window, I put out the candles and crouched in the underground storeroom where my father had kept many of his tools. Mother had never gone into the sheds, even after his death, and she didn't know of the room.

There, hiding in the dark, I had to suppress an urge to laugh. Henry and I had thought of everything. I knew that after

Herrington returned from the sheds, my mother would go into my room to see if I was there. I had arranged with Henry that he would lie in my bed so my mother would think I was asleep. Later, when I met up with Henry, we laughed when he told me of their conversation.

"Nicolas is asleep," she'd said. "It's not him."

"Well, it wasn't a thief. Nothing was taken," Herrington answered.

"What could it be? I cannot imagine anyone would go in there just to work. You don't think . . . Could it actually be Sam?"

"Lucinda, don't be silly. Perhaps we just imagined it."

A week later, we successfully pulled off another haunting, this time scaring Herrington so much that he and my mother actually discussed the possibility that my father was haunting the grounds. Henry and I then decided we would take turns in the shed. So the next night I was in my room while Henry played the role of my father's ghost.

Later that night, I listened from my room as they spoke. "Maybe I married you too quickly," my mother said to Herrington.

"No. But I don't know what we're going to do. I may have to speak to him, to this phantasm, to explain my intentions for the family," said Herrington, his voice shaking.

The next day, Henry roared with laughter as I did my impression of the scared Herrington, and we decided to continue with our haunting the following week. But it was during that third week that everything went terribly wrong and our fortunes turned for the worse.

The night was perfectly Gothic—cloudy and windy—and I was in my room waiting for Henry to start the charade. I expected that at any second I would hear the pounding of a hammer on the anvil, but minutes passed and still nothing. *What is taking him so long?* I fumed. Finally I peeked out my bedroom window and saw what looked like a red flame rising from inside the shed. What was happening?

"There's a fire—the shed is on fire!" I heard Herrington yell suddenly.

"Oh my God," Mother responded.

I ran out of my room and fell in step behind Herrington, who was already racing out the back door. When I got outside, the shed door swung open, and out ran Henry, heading towards our neighbor's property.

"Stop! I'm ordering you to stop," Herrington yelled after him. Henry darted towards a patch of overgrown bushes while I stood there frozen, just watching. I thought Herrington would reach him, but before he could, a sudden explosion of fire caught our attention and ended the chase. The wind had come in through the open shed door, fanning the fire, and now it was spreading fast to Father's other sheds.

The flames leapt onto our wooden fence and scurried towards the Allans' property, which bordered ours. The dry grass on their property led the fire to their barn, and soon the animals inside were making all sorts of horrible noises. I watched it all as if it were some dreadful dream, my inertia a result of fear and guilt. I noticed then that Herrington was running around, carrying pails of water.

Suddenly he stopped in front of me, grabbed my shoulders, and shook me. "Run over to the Allans' house—wake them," he ordered, running back towards our well again. I did as he ordered, and soon they and the other neighbors around us were helping, trying to put out the fire.

By the time the fire was extinguished, three of the Allans' cows were dead, along with several chickens and two pigs, and I too felt dead inside. Our fence and all three of Father's blacksmith sheds were destroyed.

I looked at the charred remains of Father's workplace, where he had spent so much time doing his trade, a trade he truly loved, and tears came to my eyes. It was like he had died all over again. Then I heard the sound of horses and looked up. Some officials from town were arriving. Obviously one of our neighbors had gone for help.

"There's been someone in our sheds these past three weeks," Herrington told one of the men who walked up to us. I realized then that he was a policeman.

"I wasn't sure who it was, but tonight I saw a young man run out of there," Herrington continued.

"Where did he go?" the officer asked.

"Over there," Herrington said, pointing to the bushes Henry had run to. A few of the policemen, joined by a few of our neighbors, soon began searching the bushes between us and the Allans' property. I had no idea where Henry had ended up. I just hoped that in the ruckus he had somehow managed to slip away. I looked over at Mother, whose already pale face looked ghostly in the moonlight, and felt ashamed about what had transpired.

Then one of the officers walked over to me. "What did you see?" he asked.

"The same as him," I muttered.

"Did you recognize the young man?"

The way he peered intently into my face made me very uncomfortable.

"No," I whispered.

Suddenly I heard screaming coming from the Allans' property, and three men came dragging a scared-looking Henry with them. "We found this boy hiding on our property," said Mr. Allan.

"Who the hell are you?" Herrington said. He grabbed him roughly.

"My God, that's Nic's friend—Henry," Mother said. "What are you doing here?"

"I don't care who it is. I'm going to thrash the hell out of him," Herrington yelled.

"Now wait," said the officer.

But as Herrington lunged towards Henry, I ran over. I would not let Henry take all the blame. "Let him go," I cried. "Let him go. This was my doing."

"What?" Mother asked. "What is going on?"

"It was just a prank, a joke I played on George," I admitted. "I was trying to haunt him."

"Why, Nicolas? Why would you do this?" she asked.

"I was hoping I could scare him away."

We just stared at each other. I could see the hurt in Mother's eyes, and I hated myself for what I had done.

"You lied to me, an officer of the law," the policeman said sternly.

I was silent.

"This is serious. Now you two will tell the truth."

So for the next half hour, Henry and I told our story to the grave-looking police officer. Henry told him how he had inadvertently knocked over one of the low candles in the shed, which had caught fire on some hay. Soon Henry's father appeared, looking furious.

"There could be serious charges filed here, boys," the officer said. "You started a fire, destroyed property, and killed livestock. And you," he said, glaring at me, "lied to me, and worse, pretended to be your dead father. For tonight you'll be allowed to stay with your families, but by tomorrow things may change."

As the police left, Henry and I looked at each other for just a moment before his father ordered him into the family's carriage. He looked as scared as I felt. What would happen to us? I then turned to face what I knew would be an unpleasant encounter. "Get in the house," Herrington barked.

I immediately walked in, for once respecting his orders. Mother followed behind, crying. We walked into the living room, and he turned to her. "Lucinda, let me deal with this. Do you give me permission to do what I must? It's time he learns who is now the master of this house."

"Yes. It's for the best, son," she said, looking at me with tear-filled eyes as she walked out of the room.

I felt scared then. George was a tall and strong man, with a physique built over years of rough ship labor. I was a tall but skinny teenager. I stared at him apprehensively.

"Nicolas, I am going to punish you as sailors are punished aboard my ship. Once they are punished like this, they learn to respect the order of command. I expect you will learn that I am the man of the house now, and you will respect and do as I say from now on."

"Never," I spat out. "You will never be my father."

"That may be so, but after tonight, you will learn to respect me as you did him; otherwise, there will be a painful price to pay," he said. Before I could respond, he opened a chest that sat in our living room and pulled out a short white rope that had a thick knot in it. I began to back up then, but before I knew it, he was upon me. He struck me in the face with his fist several times and then, knocking me to the floor, rolled me over and began striking me with the rope on my back, my arms, my buttocks. Try as I might to move, the pain of the lashings paralyzed me. I don't know how long it lasted. I just know that eventually he stopped and dragged me into my room, where he threw me on my bed.

The next morning, I could barely sit up; I saw with horror the bloodstains on my sheets. Then I cried from pain and shame as I pulled the tattered shirt from my torn back and stared at my cut, bruised, and swollen face in a small mirror. Herrington had beaten me, and Mother had approved it.

I spent that day in my room in bed. Mother did not come and see me, but Herrington came in once with a pitcher of water and some bread. I was too weak to say anything to him. He walked over to the bed, and for a moment I was afraid he would hit me again. Instead he looked down at me with a small, satisfied smile. "Now perhaps you'll respect me," he said, and he turned around and left.

I could not sleep that night, but instead lay there in agony. The next morning, I was still lying in bed, somewhat delirious from pain and lack of sleep, when Mother came in. Her face turned white when she saw me, but I would not say anything to her. I hated her then.

"I've come to wash your cuts," she said. I let her clean the wounds, groaning in pain as tears ran down my face, but not responding to her attempts at conversation.

"I'm sorry if this hurts, but you will survive," she said. "Please don't be angry with me." Still I said nothing, and she left the room.

A day later, I was still in bed but had begun to ponder my future. I did not want to live there anymore. I felt rage against both my mother and Herrington. How could she allow him to do this to me, to us? Father had never laid a hand on me once I turned thirteen, and this animal had brutally beaten me.

I thought then of Father, of how kind he'd always been. Even when he had disciplined me, he had always spoken kindly with me afterward, explaining why. Now Mother was married to this man who acted like a brute. How could she marry such a monster? I knew there was still nearly a month to go before George headed off on his next whaling trip, and I didn't think I could stand it. I had to leave home. I would have to run away. Maybe Henry could help, but that would have to wait until I healed and was stronger. I didn't want Henry to see what George had done to me. It made me feel weak.

The next day, though, I heard a low tapping on my bedroom window. I slowly sat up but saw no one. Then I saw a hand come up out of the bushes that bordered the bottom of my windowsill. The hand rapped against the pane again. "Nic, it's me. Let me in." It was Henry's muffled voice.

"Go away. I can't see you," I yelled.

"Open the window. George and your mother aren't home. I saw them leave, but I didn't want your neighbors telling them I'd come over, so I snuck through the back. I'm in a heap of trouble as it is, and the longer I stay out here, the more likely I'll be seen." He stood up then, looked into my room at me, and gasped.

I turned away.

"Open up," he repeated.

"Fine," I grumbled, turning around to open the window.

"My God," he said as he crawled in. "George did that?"

I just turned away again.

"What a bastard," Henry said. "I'm sorry."

We were silent for a minute, and then Henry spoke again. "Well, my father didn't lay a hand on me; he's just ruining my life."

"What do you mean?" I asked, finally turning to face him.

"Father believes a voyage aboard a sea vessel is what every boy needs to become a man. It was what made him strong, brave, and able, he said. Actually, he's been telling the story of his experiences aboard the *Sonnet Seas* for as long as I can remember. It was there that he learned everything he needed to know in life, he says—how to make money, gain respect, love a woman, and fight hard. I've heard this story for so long that my attention wanders when he begins repeating it. But the night of the fire, he was so furious, he said my actions had convinced him that I need to become a man. He says that Mother has coddled all of us children too much. Except the rest are girls and I'm a boy, so guess who's being shipped off to become a man. Much to my dismay, he signed me up for a whaling voyage."

"What?"

"Yes. I leave in three weeks. He worked out a deal with Captain Laughlin of the *Mary Selina*. It's one of Father's ships."

"I don't understand it," I said. "It seems extreme."

"Well, look at you," Henry said, smirking.

"I suppose."

"You don't know what's been going on, do you?"

"I've been insensible the last few days," I admitted.

"Well, they talked about jailing both of us, but then Father paid for the damages to the Allans' barns and for the loss of their animals, and he told the authorities he would punish me severely. I guess George must have told them you were beaten, so they decided against arresting us. I've been wondering what happened to you."

He looked me over again and shook his head. "Bastard," he said. "I could kill him."

"That would only make matters worse," I said.

"Well, I don't know which one of us is luckier. I'm being sent to work as a deckhand. Can you imagine how they're going to treat me, the owner's son? They'll probably make this some sort of hell, with my father's permission. I hate to say this, Nic, but I'd almost prefer your punishment. God, I do not want to go," he said, lowering his face into his hands. I didn't know what to say, so instead I just put my hand on his back. "What are you going to do now?" he asked, looking up.

"I hate them both right now. She let him do this. Maybe we can run away together."

"And do what? If I run away, I'll be disowned. I can't do that," he said.

"Well, I'm not staying here. Every time I hear George's voice, I feel ill. I can't stay."

"Well then, maybe you should come with me."

I looked up at him.

"That's it," he said, suddenly looking cheerful. "You can join the crew too. I'll talk to Father if you'd like."

"I don't know," I said.

"Come on. Why not go on an adventure with your best friend?"

And so our fate was set.

Three and a half weeks later, we both shipped off on the *Mary Selina*. George and Mother had agreed it was best for me, and I left the house that morning without saying good-bye to either of them. I regret that now, not for Herrington, of course, but for Mother. Before marrying him, she had always been kind to me, and looking back, I realize that I had deserved some sort of punishment, and she had probably not known her new husband would be so brutal. But I didn't know I'd never see her again.

CHAPTER 4

Henry and I walked towards the ship together that morning to face our future. He, of course, as the ship owner's son, was better prepared. While his finely stocked sea chest was being delivered aboard, I toted a white duffel bag with a few items of clothing, toiletries, and my sketchbook, pencils, and charcoals. The wharf was brimming with excitement and life. During the past two weeks, over a dozen ships had already left port.

Before we left, Henry's father had spelled out all the details of the trip to us. We would probably be gone for about two years on this hunt, which was to take us out and down the coast of South America. We would head west round the tip of Cape Horn and then north again before returning. Two years! It seemed such a long time to me. When we returned, we'd both be nearly eighteen and not the boys we were now.

I was nervous as Henry and I boarded and first saw those who were now our shipmates. Most of the men looked older than us. I guessed that they were in their twenties and thirties, although some were even older. Looking over them, I could see that there was quite a mix of humanity aboard this ship. Along with us Yankees, black and white, were some Portuguese, a

Peruvian, and several Europeans. I later found out that our crew numbered twenty-three.

Henry and I just stood there, not knowing who to talk to or what to do. Then we noticed a broad-shouldered, dark-bearded man heading straight towards us.

"I'm Captain Samuel Laughlin," he said, looking us over from foot to head and back down again. It made me uncomfortable. "Hmph," he said. "Nicolas Adams and Master Henry Lawton. A weak couple of deckhands you make. A little too skinny, but you're both tall. I guess you'll have to do."

He then walked off.

Later, Denny Reilly, one of the younger crew members, explained that the captain was sizing up our physical status to see where we might be valuable. We were of course green hands, inexperienced, and we would be forced to learn quickly once we were out at sea, but on the day we sailed away from New Bedford, we had what I consider the honeymoon period of our sailing adventure.

As we clipped along on a stiff breeze, I became enthralled with the nature that surrounded us—the deep aqua sea; the endless, expanding sky; the fish that sometimes leapt out from the sea—but what I think I enjoyed most was the feeling of freedom. My freedom from Herrington and the freedom of leaving land and casting our fates to pure nature. "I think we did the right thing," I said to Henry, who seemed lost in his own reverie. "I can't wait to create some sketches of all this."

"Yes, this will be fun," he answered. Unfortunately, we were both wrong.

CHAPTER 5

If I were asked to give four short descriptions of life aboard the *Mary Selina*, it would be these: the foulest of stenches, the most disgusting food, the hardest of backbreaking work, and the majesty of an endless ocean. I'll start with the positive. The ocean is a radiant queen whose beauty is unparalleled. There is nothing that compares to watching the massive red orb of the sun melt into the horizon, spreading its brightness into the water. Nothing compares to riding aboard a ship with a brisk wind propelling it such that you feel as if you're flying. There is nothing as exciting as being graced with the unexpected appearance of a magnificent creature like a whale or dolphin or sea turtle.

All of this I loved about being at sea, but there was much I hated. While the *Mary Selina* was a beauty, her stench could be assailing. How to describe it? It was a smell of the sea, of animals, fish, and even the people onboard, all of which combined to become the most offensive trail one could imagine. The worst was the bilgewater that gathered around the pumps. It retained the most noxious scent, which caused even the older sea hands to vomit as they worked the pumps. Neither soap nor rags could keep a mariner smelling good when he was out at sea aboard a whaler, often using seawater to bathe with, if he bathed at all. So Henry and I also became rancid, and it was strange for me to see and smell him that way. At home he had always been so groomed, so clean, so—well, perfect.

Then there was the work. At fifteen, Henry and I were the youngest and most inexperienced aboard the *Mary Selina*. The other sailors were men who had already spent most of their lives at sea, and they were experienced in ship work. And so to us fell the lowliest of tasks. Being a foremast hand, I decided, was much like being a slave. It was we who scrubbed and swept the decks of the blood of slaughtered animals and fish and other nasty fluids. We also brought food to the captain and the first mate and some of the other senior crew, and then cleaned up after them. Whenever I had the time, which was rare, to talk to Henry, all I did was complain:

"Did you see the cockroaches in the molasses?"

"The heat and filth of the forecastle is unbearable."

"Now I've got fleas."

But Henry never complained. He seemed to take it all in stride.

We quickly learned to climb, to repair sails, to coil stray lines, and to find sleep when and where we could, because rest was a luxury. We had to serve four-hour watch shifts on deck, with only a few hours of sleep in between. On some days, Henry and I barely spoke, just crawled past each other, exhausted, to lie down in our tiny bunks in the crawl space of the forecastle. Still, as rough as it all was, there was another positive: our shared misery brought Henry and me even closer than we already were. We would look at each other and almost instinctively know what the other was thinking and feeling. Henry was my confidant, my friend, and the only person I trusted and relied on aboard the ship.

One night I was so nervous that even though I was exhausted, I couldn't fall asleep, but kept tossing and turning, and it woke Henry out of his sound sleep.

"What's the matter?" he asked.

"I'm worried about tomorrow. I don't think I can go up to the crow's nest."

"If I can do it, you can do it," he answered. "It's actually quite exhilarating to be up there."

A week earlier, Henry had been ordered the watch in the crow's nest, and I had stared in amazement as he scurried up the rope ladder we had learned to call ratlines, as if he had done it all his life. Then I remembered how athletic he'd always been—running faster than any of the boys we'd raced, swimming farther out into the sea than anyone I'd known, and catching baseballs with the greatest of ease.

"You'll be fine," he said.

I wasn't so sure, and I spent the night drifting in and out of an uneasy sleep. The next morning, I walked out to the deck as if I were walking to my own hanging. There was no way I could get out of this. On a ship, an order is followed or, as Herrington had taught me, there is a painful price to pay. So I slowly headed towards the ratlines and began my clumsy climb.

For a while, it seemed I would make it, then suddenly I slipped. A fall to the deck meant your certain demise, and so I clung to the line with a death grip, sweating and cursing. Below I heard crew members laughing, and I realized they were watching me. I was so embarrassed. Then, out from the noise of the laughter, I heard Henry's voice.

"Shut up, you idiots," he yelled. "Keep going, Nicolas; you can do it. Remember how we climbed onto the roof of the Roderick manor. Remember. This is nothing."

He was right. *I can do this,* I tried to convince myself. I slowly continued up and finally made it to the crow's nest, which was nothing but a large barrel lashed to the highest mast of the ship. I thought the worst would be over once I'd dragged myself into the barrel, but I was wrong. When I stood up, I found myself becoming dizzy, then nauseous. After a few minutes, I was seasick, throwing up over the side of the barrel.

I heard the crew laughing again, but I was too sick to care. All I knew was that I was too dizzy to move. I can't say that I really did any kind of watch up there under the circumstances, but the time passed, and eventually it was time for me to come down. But I wasn't budging. I was still dizzy and terrified of falling.

"Nic, you've got to come down."

That was Henry's voice again, but this time he sounded nearby. I peered over the barrel to see him climbing up the ratlines. He had come to help me.

"I'm too sick," I muttered. "I'll fall."

"No. You'll be fine. I'll talk you down. We'll go down together, slowly. Just listen to my voice. Do what I tell you to do."

So that's what I did. Painstakingly, slowly, step by step, Henry talked me down the ladder, and we made it back to the deck—to be greeted again by laughter.

"*Que bello*," said Marco, the Peruvian, with a wink. "How lovely to watch *esta niña* saved by his *amigo*."

"Oh, a lovely pair these two make," added John, who at age thirty had spent half of his life at sea.

"Just leave 'em alone," said Denny, who was one of the few crew members to treat us with any respect.

By now they'd all heard our story about how we'd ended up on the ship, and they treated us with a sort of disdain, mocking our lack of sailing knowledge. As much as we attempted to learn the ropes—literally—we knew it might take us years. Each line that supported the spars or controlled the sails had a different name. How would we ever learn what went where and controlled what? How would we ever get the others to treat us better? We had to call them "sir," and if they felt we weren't respecting them or were taking too long to do something, they would sometimes lash out.

Well, not at Henry, but at me. I paid for not only my own clumsiness and errors but for Henry's errors too. At first I wondered why, but then the truth struck me. The crew must have been told to keep their hands off of him, the ship owner's son, and so it was I who took the brunt of everything. I soon learned that Herrington's beating had perhaps been a favor, preparing me for what lay ahead. While none of the crew's hits yet had been as painful as his, they did leave me resentful, and for the first time in my life, I found myself at times angry at Henry—not for something he had done, but for the advantages of who he was. The advantages that I knew he knew existed, but that we wouldn't discuss, at least not yet. Still, it was hard to stay angry at Henry. He had always come through for me.

CHAPTER 6

By our fifth week out, the hard labor had weakened me, and I came down with a sore throat, which turned into a fever that left me unfit for duty. For days I lay on my cot, shaking with cold, then burning with heat, and at times even delirious. I don't remember much, only that when my fever finally broke for good and I returned to my senses, I discovered Henry sitting near me, his eyes bloodshot and his face drawn.

"What happened?" I muttered weakly.

"You've been really ill, Nic. For a while I wasn't sure if you were going to live."

"Really? I've been that sick?"

"You were burning up," he said. I noticed then that Henry was holding my hand. He noticed that I was looking and let it go.

"I'm just glad you're okay now," he said. "I don't think I could survive here without you."

I was still so weak that it was a few days before I could return to duty. But when I did return, I was surprised, because I was given much shorter watch shifts. Perhaps the captain had somehow taken pity on me, or perhaps he didn't want me to get ill again, because every hand on a ship is needed. But now, for the first time in over a month, I actually had a little free time. The first thing I did was pull out my sketchbook to draw, envisioning in my head some of the sights I'd seen in the past weeks. As I sketched my memory of two dolphins that had followed our ship for miles, I looked up at Denny, who had wandered over to see what I was drawing.

"That's pretty good," he said, "but you might enjoy what they're looking at over there."

I looked back to see two of the crew bent over something they were passing back and forth. Curiosity got the best of me, so I went to see what they were looking at. I peered down and felt blood rushing into my face. They were staring at daguerreotypes of naked women. I had never seen such images and couldn't help but stare myself. I wondered where they'd gotten them; probably at some port town, where they had obviously gone to the houses of ill repute. New Bedford had its share of such places, but I had come aboard the ship relatively innocent, and my eyes and ears were now awakening to that part of life. I'd listened for weeks now to men sharing bawdy portside stories, seen some of the men naked during the rare times they'd wash themselves, and I even listened to men breathing hard and sometimes groaning as they pleasured themselves, their bunks so close to mine and Henry's.

"You're curious, eh?"

It was Henry's voice, and he was walking towards us. I felt my face flush even more.

"I've already seen them," Henry snickered.

CHAPTER 7

My week of short shifts went by quickly, and before I knew it, I was back to the same routine of hard labor and endless abuse. One person who seemed to pick on both Henry and me more than the others was the oldest man on the ship. With his white hair, shrunken physique, and frail disposition, Jeremiah McGuire was a bit of a mystery. What sort of captain would recruit such a man for such a physical type of job? McGuire would often fall asleep on watch and have to be awakened by others. We never really saw him contribute to any of the work that was required to keep the ship afloat; instead, he seemed to just stand around, watching and commenting on what others were doing and criticizing everyone. In particular, he liked to lash out at me, balling up a rope in his hands, as Herrington had, to make his strikes more painful than they otherwise would have been from his old and shrunken hands. Although McGuire, like the others, never hit Henry, he would curse at him in the harshest ways.

One day, about a month after I recovered from the fever, McGuire was especially tough on me, and after several hours of both verbal and physical abuse, I ran away to stop myself from striking back at him. I knew I would be punished for leaving my duty, but the punishment would be much worse if I dared strike a senior shipmate. As I crawled back into the forecastle and waited to see who would come to retrieve me, a sense of hopelessness descended upon me. I wondered why I had ever agreed to join Henry on this supposed "adventure," and I suddenly felt horribly homesick for New Bedford. Then my eyes filled with tears I had thought long gone, especially after these past months, which I believed had noticeably hardened me.

When I heard footsteps behind me, I quickly brushed my tears from my eyes, worried that someone would see my sudden weakness.

"Are you okay?"

It was Henry.

"Fine," I muttered.

"But you're crying," Henry said.

"Get out, Henry," I said, horribly embarrassed.

"I don't blame you for being upset. That bastard is an idiot. I can't stand the way he treats you. It makes me want to kill him."

"Don't talk like that. You know what it could lead to if someone heard."

"I don't care, Nic. I won't allow him to continue. You're everyth—" He stopped. "Well, I just can't stand it," he continued, and then he reached his arms out and hugged me.

At first I didn't mind Henry's touch, the feel of his body against mine, his right hand dropping to the small of my back. But then my breathing quickened, and my body tingled, and I was getting an erection. What was wrong with me? This wasn't right. I pulled away, pushing Henry off of me.

"Go away, Henry," I said, my face burning in humiliation. I hoped he hadn't noticed.

"Nic, I . . . well, I'm here for you if you need me," Henry said awkwardly. "I have to go back. I just came to tell you that Thompson said you could take the rest of the shift off."

"Why would he do that?" I asked.

Cleophat Thompson, the captain's first mate, didn't believe in second chances. He was a hulk of a man, a handsome, strapping figure with thick red hair and bright green eyes. Even though he was only twenty-eight, Thompson had already spent sixteen years at sea and was one of the most able seamen aboard the ship. One of Thompson's jobs was to enforce discipline, so we usually kept out of his way and sight. But now he seemed to be going easy on me.

"Believe it or not, they're not all bad, Nic," Henry said, walking away.

As Henry left, I doubled over in disgust with myself. What was wrong with me? How could I feel that way about Henry? They were sinful feelings, and I hoped they would never return. I remembered the many evenings my father had read passages from the Bible aloud to me and Mother. Once he had read from Leviticus: "Do not lie with a man as one lies with a woman."

Perhaps it's just this ship, these tight quarters, I told myself. *Perhaps I'm just going crazy.*

That night, when Henry returned to lie near me in the forecastle, I turned away from him, not wanting to see him there in all his handsomeness. I fell into a troubled sleep that was filled with images of blood and water.

CHAPTER 8

Two days later, while we swept the deck, McGuire was up to his usual harassment. When he walked away, Henry said loudly, "He's an old fool whose time is coming."

"Shh," I admonished him.

But it was too late.

"You boys would do well not to complain about McGuire."

We looked back, fearing the worst. We were lucky that day. It was only Denny.

"Why does he have it out for us?" Henry asked. "We're tired of his harassment."

"As the oldest aboard, McGuire feels his role is disciplinarian," Denny said. "But like I said, don't speak poorly about him. McGuire is the captain's uncle, and the captain doesn't take too kindly to any complaints about the old man. You see, when the captain's mother was on her deathbed, she pleaded with Captain Laughlin to take her brother on his voyages. She was worried about what would become of him, because of, well, you know."

Like the others, we had come to know that McGuire was not only angry and useless, but illiterate and superstitious.

Around his neck he wore a chain, at its end a scrimshaw piece etched with a mermaid. Whenever a storm came, McGuire would rub the scrimshaw and whisper, "Protect us, maiden of the seas. Protect our lives. Protect our ship." Henry and I had laughed at this peculiar habit and begun imitating the man whenever we saw storm clouds or felt threatened in any way.

Well, one night McGuire's luck seemed to run out. He fell asleep on watch, and this time none of the other crew members woke him. Instead, he was discovered by Thompson. The next day, in front of all of us, Thompson whipped the old man twice on the shoulders. This seemed to contradict what Denny had told us earlier. "Isn't Thompson afraid of the captain's reaction?" I whispered to Denny as we stood and watched the violent spectacle.

"Thompson is the only one the captain allows to discipline his uncle. Thompson has been the captain's first mate for the past six years now and is his closest confidant."

Of course the weak old man collapsed. Thompson turned to where the crew stood watching. "You, Henry," he said.

"Yes," Henry answered nervously.

"Come help me take him to his bunk."

Up to that point, our contact with Thompson had been rare, but after that, this changed. Several days after McGuire's beating, Thompson appeared on deck one night to join us and the other crew members while we talked and sang. We were even more surprised when he started to make it a habit to join us at least one night a week. Then his behavior became even odder.

"He what?" I asked.

"He wants us to come over to his cabin tonight when we're both off watch."

"Why?"

"I don't know. He said we could play cards."

It made me uncomfortable, for I'd always thought his recent friendliness was an act. And why would a superior officer, older than us, want us in his room? I shook off my thoughts. Maybe I was just not being clearheaded about the situation. I had suspected that perhaps Thompson was spying for the captain, reporting our words and actions, so when I was around him, I was always careful. Maybe this invitation was a way of getting us away from our crewmates so he could ask us questions about them.

I didn't trust Thompson, but Henry did. Perhaps because he always treated Henry in a kindly manner, while with me he was cold and rude. I detected a strange loathing from him that I couldn't understand and felt his friendly manners towards Henry were related to the special privileges Henry received from all of the crew. Thompson, like the others, knew that Henry was the son of the ship's owner. He was perhaps trying to cultivate a close friendship for his own interests.

However, despite all my conflicting suspicions, I couldn't just ignore a request from a superior, so that night Henry and I headed to Thompson's cabin, which was located in the stern of the ship.

"Welcome, boys," he said, escorting us in.

While Thompson's cabin was small and held just a narrow bed, a sea chest, a table, and a few chairs, he lived like a king compared to most of us crew, who slept cramped together in the forecastle. "Sit," Thompson said, pointing to the table and chairs. Upon the table were a deck of cards, three glasses and plates, a knife, a block of fresh white cheese, and a bottle of amber-colored liquid. Thompson offered us the cheese, and after so many meals of hard tack and stale bread, it tasted like heaven.

"So tell me about yourselves, boys," he said. "How did you become friends?"

We told him how we'd met by the wharf as kids and found a common bond in playing jokes. Then Thompson told us more about himself, and I began to understand why Henry liked him. Thompson's handsome face lit up when he shared the stories of all the ports he had been to during his life at sea. Really, it was a rather remarkable life. He told us about the retired pirates he'd tangled with in Jamaica; the story writer he drank shots with in Shanghai; and a treacherous preacher who confessed a sordid story of debauchery in Argentina.

"Have you boys drunk much?" he asked, pouring the amber-colored liquid into the glasses. "I thought you might want some."

Henry took a swig, and I saw him shudder slightly; my curiosity got the better of me, and I decided to try it too. I coughed and gagged, much to the amusement of both Thompson and Henry. Rum was strong.

Thompson picked up the cards and taught Henry and me this game called Stud Poker, which I had never played before and wouldn't play well that night, for within the hour, both Henry and I were drunk. For me it was just an overwhelming feeling of sleepiness and numbness that took hold, and I could barely hold up my hand of cards. But the alcohol seemed to have a different effect on Henry. He became obnoxious, rattling on about our adventures in New Bedford and giggling like some silly schoolgirl. When we finally left, I decided that perhaps drinking wasn't for me. After all, I hadn't really enjoyed the taste, and now I could barely walk back to my bunk.

The next week Thompson invited us again, but I didn't want to go. My back was hurting from a day spent scrubbing the decks. Yet I knew I couldn't refuse his request, so I forced myself to go along with Henry. As we stood outside, waiting for Thompson to open the door to his cabin, Henry glanced over at me.

"What's wrong?" he asked, noticing what I guessed was a scowl on my face.

"I guess I'm just tired," I said, as the door opened.

"You don't have to join us," said Thompson, who had obviously overheard my comment. He looked as if we had interrupted his undressing. His white shirt was unbuttoned nearly to his navel, exposing what looked to be a well-chiseled chest. "Henry and I can play alone."

"All right then," I said, glancing over at Henry, who was staring at Thompson and seemed oblivious to my presence. The situation didn't feel right somehow—I didn't want to leave Henry alone with Thompson—but it felt too awkward to change my mind, so I headed back to the forecastle.

I was fast asleep when a sudden jolt to my bunk drove me awake. I was immediately assailed with the scent of rum and noticed Henry standing over me. He was disheveled, his shirt hanging out from his trousers, the top few buttons of his pants unhooked. He looked messy, but beautiful, and I tried to push the thought out of my head even as I found myself aroused again. I wouldn't allow myself to feel that, so instead I sat up in a rage. "What happened to you?" I whispered angrily, not wanting to wake anyone up.

"Oops, sorry." Henry's words came out loudly and slurred. "I didn't see you there, Nic."

"Quiet, lads," one of our mates yelled out.

"Sorry," Henry said, leaning down closer to me. "You missed out on some good food and drink tonight. It was a good time."

"Like that bastard cares if I'm there," I snapped.

"He's quite charming, you know," Henry said. "He talks a lot to me."

"About what?"

"About his life and mine, my father, the captain, the ship and—" He stopped, and I noticed he was staring at me. "Does it bother you?" he asked. "You seem angry."

"Well yes," I said roughly. There was an odd gleam of satisfaction in his eyes. "I don't trust him, Henry. You need to be careful."

"Don't worry, Nic. No matter what happens, you know I will always side with you. We've known each other too long and been through too much. Now good night," he said, and crawled into his bunk.

In my heart I knew that nothing could separate us, but my head was filled with troubling thoughts of Thompson and Henry. Had they kissed? Touched each other? It wasn't right. Upset about that, and about my own wrong feelings for Henry, I fell into a troubled sleep.

CHAPTER 9

Life aboard the whaler had settled into a harsh but by now familiar routine, although the situation with Henry festered like some slow-healing sore. We were just past the Windward Islands, headed south and nearing the northern coast of South America. I was no longer invited to Thompson's cabin, and I had to tamp down my feelings every week when Henry took leave to go see him. Frankly, it sickened me when I imagined them together. He was older than us, our superior, and I believed he had seduced Henry, but a part of me was afraid to find out the truth. I couldn't ask Henry straight out. If it was true, then Thompson was a monster, and what they were doing was sinful, but what I wanted was just as sinful, so I forced myself to put my energies elsewhere.

Whenever Henry left, I would pull out my sketchbook and pencils and focus on capturing the marvelous nature, which seemed to be the only enjoyment I had from this God-awful voyage. My art was a respite; I found comfort in the rhythm of sketching, in the motion of the pencils scraping back and forth on the paper. Nothing in my prior experiences could compare with the beauty of watching the enormous red sun dissolve into the sea at night, or seeing a pod of dolphins leap gracefully alongside our ship, or watching the flight of a manta ray under the waves. Some of the other men would sometimes peek over my shoulder and compliment my efforts to capture these scenes, and it made me feel good. Then Henry would come back from his time with Thompson, and I would feel ill with worry.

"Is he hurting you?" I asked him one time, when he came back drunk again.

He looked over at me and smirked. "You'll never understand it, Nic. You're just not there yet."

He was right. I didn't understand. "Henry, something's not right," I said.

"Shut the hell up, Nic!" The fury of his tone surprised and silenced me. "You can't understand this," he continued.

Perhaps not, I thought. But I feared for Henry, and I wondered why our friendship couldn't be enough for him.

Then, on my sixteenth birthday, I had a most amazing spiritual experience.

It had been another sweltering day. We were just south of the equator, with a ways to go yet before rounding Cape Horn and heading north towards our final destination, which was just west of Peru—a spot that decades earlier had been discovered to be prime sperm-whale hunting ground. I was alone on deck; it must have been about two in the morning, and at a far distance, I saw what I thought to be a lone whale breaching the waves, as if trying to ascend into the heavens in a vain attempt to escape its watery realm. I knew I should report it, probably right away—after all, we were searching for whales. But I didn't. I made up my mind then that I was not interested in killing such magnificent creatures.

I thought the sight of the whale was perhaps the beginning to a fortuitous day, but I was wrong about that. Later that day, as I weaved my way past some barrels on deck, I tripped over a line that lay sprawled across the path. Most unfortunate for me, McGuire happened to be walking towards me at that very moment. As I fell forward, I reached out to catch myself and landed right on McGuire, my hand inadvertently swiping his chest and breaking the chain he wore with his scrimshaw mermaid. The scrimshaw piece flew off the ship and into the sea.

McGuire's reaction was instantaneous. "What have you done? You have doomed us all," he screamed, pushing me off of him and onto the deck.

"We're doomed, we're doomed," he began yelling. "We're doomed!"

Everyone began staring at us, and the ruckus he caused eventually brought the captain out from below deck, followed by others, including Thompson and Henry.

"What's going on here?" the captain bellowed. "What in God's name is this talk of doom?"

I stood tongue-tied and silent as McGuire told him how I had tripped and made him lose the mermaid that watched over the ship.

"I fear that now we will be lost by a storm or attacked by a whale," McGuire said.

"Now, now, Jeremiah. Calm down, calm down," the captain said, looking slightly red-faced at his relative's outburst. "I'm sure that God has blessed this ship, scrimshaw mermaid or not. Now go below and get some rest. I will take care of the boy.

"Stoppard," he yelled to the nearest crewman. "Take Jeremiah below and make sure he settles down."

When the old man was gone, the captain turned to me. His face was red and his eyes blazing. "Your clumsiness, boy, has caused quite a ruckus this morning. Whose job is it to make sure there are no stray lines that can cause dangerous accidents?"

"Mine and Henry's," I said quietly.

"That's right, yours. This is a danger to everyone aboard the ship. Someone tripping over a line might fall overboard. For this you will be punished. Thompson, flog the boy."

Upon those words, I received the second-worst and perhaps the most humiliating beating of my life. At least with Herrington, no one, not even my mother, had watched, but as Thompson pulled my shirt off my shoulders, all the others stood around and watched. Worst of all, try as I might to stifle any reaction, I couldn't help but cry out as the cat-o'-nine-tails tore into my shoulders and back. When it was done, I could barely stand, and a white-faced Henry rushed to me and helped me below deck, where I fell down.

"Bastards, all of them," Henry snarled. "Especially that dunce McGuire. I will get back at him for you, Nicolas. I promise."

"What about Thompson? I bet he enjoyed it," I protested weakly.

"Of course I'll say something to him. Although he has to follow the captain's orders, there was no reason for him to tear you up this way. But it started with that idiot McGuire, and he will pay for this."

His words were dangerous, but I was too weak to protest any further, and I spent the rest of the day in my bunk. I awoke in the middle of the night to discover Henry limping into the forecastle. His shirt was torn, and as he neared, I noticed that it looked like he too had been beaten. One of his eyes was puffy, and his bottom lip was bleeding.

"What happened?" I whispered.

"It's nothing," he said.

"Tell me," I pressed, suddenly realizing. "It was Thompson, wasn't it?"

"Yes. Yes. I told him that what he did to you was unacceptable. That our relation—our friendship was over. And he didn't take it well. He attacked me."

"You need to tell the captain," I said. "You need to tell him everything. What he did to you, what he's done . . ."

"No, no no!" Henry interrupted, his eyes welling up with tears. "It's nothing. And it's all over now."

But I wasn't so sure if that was true, and it terrified me to think that Thompson, who had already taken advantage of Henry in so many ways, might turn even more violent.

CHAPTER 10

The next day, neither I nor Henry had time to think about Thompson or McGuire. It was the day the crew had looked forward to for months.

It started when one of the lookouts bellowed, "Bloo-oowwwws." He had spotted a whale spout, and from then on, the hunt was on. The creature was, of course, of great value to us. Its blubber could be turned into valuable oil, while the spermaceti could be used for oil, for making candles, and for medicinal purposes such as softening skin and curing tumors. Finally, there was the whale's ambergris, which would sell for thousands of dollars and was valued around the world for use in foods, drinks, and perfumes.

Before us swam our fortune, and we quickly prepared three whaleboats for the crews that would go out on the hunt. Henry and I helped remove the sheaths from the harpoon heads, load the harpoon lines, and sharpen the irons. Then three crews, of six men each, climbed into the whaleboats, which were lowered off the starboard and the port sides of the ship, and the chase began in earnest.

Henry and I watched in anticipation of our first hunt ever, Henry pacing angrily. He was disappointed we had not been picked to be on one of the crews that manned the thirty-foot whaleboats. I didn't tell Henry that I felt relieved. I had long before decided that I didn't want to kill a mighty whale, and living in a whaling town, I had always known that whale hunting was a particularly dangerous business.

Growing up, I had heard some of the seamen's tales of horror and adventure, but because I had expected to follow in my father's land-based trade, I had believed there would be no such adventures as part of my future. Then, during all the months aboard the ship, I heard yet more frightening tales of whale hunts from some of the seasoned mariners, and I realized that the danger could become my reality. Injured and angry whales had been known to kill and maim mariners by using their massive tails and jaws as weapons, splintering whaleboats and sending mariners airborne. That was a danger I'd rather not face.

I was also troubled by my hidden feelings that killing these glorious creatures was an affront to our maker. Sperm whales in particular were magnificent beasts; the males could reach sixty feet in length and weigh up to fifty tons. When their lofty tails lifted from the sea, they reminded me of some marvelous winged bird rising from the depths. Their heads were enormous, and I had heard they were noisy creatures too, making clicking sounds that sounded like hammers through the hull of the ship. While to me whales had become a symbol of nature at its best, Henry, I knew, felt differently, and he had been scowling ever since the boats were lowered that day.

"Lucky fools," he said. "Damn Father. I'm sure he told them not to allow me on the boats."

"You're probably right," I said. "But I wonder why they spared me the task?"

"It's probably because the captain thinks you're too clumsy."

"He told you that?" I asked, surprised.

"No, it was Thompson who told me. But don't worry, my friend; I stood up for you. What he thinks no longer matters."

The hunt lasted hours, but finally we were "victorious," and the crew returned, hauling their colossal victim. I was horrified at the procedure that followed, but I kept my feelings to myself; they were emotions I feared no normal whaling man should have.

The noble creature was secured along the starboard side of our ship, with its tail facing forward. Then Captain Laughlin and Thompson walked across one of the several wooden platforms set up to traverse the creature's body, and the captain began sawing off the monumental head while Thompson began peeling off the blubber.

What followed were gut-wrenching days filled with blubber and oil. I often retched as I was forced to mop up what seemed an endless stream of blood, while watching massive blubber pieces slide across a greasy deck. Just over a week later, the filthy deed was done; our casks were filled with whale oil; and we, the crew, were grotesque and fetid. I felt as if we'd slipped into the depths of Hell, and my mood was just as foul.

One day, noticing my bad mood as I once again mopped the deck, McGuire again began picking on me in front of the crew. "Oh, does the princess not like being filthy? What a girl you are, Nicolas. What a little girl. I've watched you all these days and I can't believe the weakling you are. Your mother would be ashamed."

"You bastard," I snapped. "Just shut up."

"Hold your tongue, old man," Henry yelled, rushing to my side.

"How dare you speak to me like that, boy," McGuire said, turning on Henry. "You're nothing but a Molly yourself, and you know it. Perhaps that's why you two are such good friends," he said, bursting into cruel laughter.

I saw Henry's face blanch with embarrassment, and suddenly I could stand it no longer. I dropped my mop and flung myself at the old man, punching him in the jaw. "I will kill you," I yelled.

I suddenly found myself laid out on the deck. Thompson had heard the ruckus and taken me down with a strike across the side of the head.

"Don't worry, Nic," Henry whispered as he helped me up. "McGuire is finished. He'll never hurt us again."

"Don't be crazy," I said.

That night I was awakened by Henry, who stood over me and whispered, "Come on, follow me."

"I'm tired, Henry. Can't whatever this is wait?"

"Shh," he admonished. "Don't talk so loud. You might wake the others."

"What is it?"

"Just follow me. This might be our only chance."

Now I was curious, so I jumped up and followed him up to the deck. It was a cold and windy night, and the ship rolled jarringly as we rounded a corner. Henry stopped at one of the longboats that was in need of repairs, lying upside down on deck.

"Help me lift this," Henry said.

"What?" I wondered if Henry was losing his mind.

"Come on, do it," he said. "You'll see why."

So together we pushed up one side of the boat, and when I glimpsed underneath, I suddenly understood. There lay McGuire, sleeping huddled in sheets. The old man's eyes opened as he felt the cold, wet air assail his bower of slumber. He almost yelled out, but before he could, Henry was upon him, covering his mouth with his hand, so that only muffled groans of protest could be heard as he squiggled under Henry's grip. It was a fight he would not win. The weakened muscle of the old was no match for the strength of youth. Henry leaned down until their faces nearly touched.

"So, neglecting your duty again, old man," Henry hissed. "Don't worry, I won't tell Thompson. That's not what I'm here for. I'm here for this."

He pressed his body down upon our nemesis to keep him pinned, then released one hand and reached to grab something that, along with McGuire, had been lying underneath the boat. With horror I realized it was a Temple toggle harpoon, the long, sickle-like weapon with a sharp front point and two protruding curved points that the crew used to kill whales. I wondered how the weapon had gotten there, and then I realized that somehow Henry must have seen McGuire going underneath the boat and let the old man fall asleep, only to set the weapon near him later.

"What are you doing?" I asked, panicking as I saw Henry put the tip on McGuire's throat. The frightened man's eyes bulged. Henry just turned to me and shook his head as if to quiet me.

"Old man, you will never humiliate or hit Nic or me again, or I swear I'll slit your throat as you sleep," he snarled. "And don't think I won't do it. I'll just throw your body overboard afterwards and say there was an accident. They'll believe me. After all, you're just a doddering old superstitious fool, and I, after all, am the ship owner's son. Do you understand that?"

There was only silence.

"Answer me," Henry growled.

McGuire's mouth was still covered. He slowly moved his head up and down.

"Now. I'll let you go, but one word out of you about this and I'll just deny it. And you'll be dead."

I feared the worst would happen, that somehow McGuire would talk anyway, and I was both right and wrong. For as Henry released his grip on McGuire's mouth, the old man began yelling, but then the ship took a sharp roll, and the harpoon in Henry's hand inadvertently lunged into McGuire's neck. Henry jumped back and dropped the weapon in horror as a stream of blood spurted out of McGuire's neck while he gurgled and choked.

I foolishly attempted to help by trying to stem the tide of blood with my hands. But it was no use; he bled out as we both stood there, shocked. Then there were footsteps, and before Henry or I could react, other crew were there yelling. They knocked me off of the old man and restrained me on the deck.

"I didn't do this," I said. "It was an accident."

I wanted to tell them the accident was Henry's fault, but I couldn't. He was my best friend. No, he was more. He was everything. I remained silent.

"Like hell it wasn't your fault," said Denny. "Everyone heard you earlier, and you were on top of him when we got here. Go wake the captain," he ordered the other men who had gathered around us. As I lay forcibly held to the deck, I glanced over at Henry, who seemed to have gone into some sort of shock.

That night I was thrown unceremoniously into a storage hold, which was then locked. I couldn't sleep for wondering what awaited me.

The next morning, I was marched up to the deck, wearing chains around my wrists and ankles. I saw Henry's pale and drawn face peering out from among all the other crew gathered on the deck. There, before all the other men, I was accused of being a murderer, and Captain Laughlin read my punishment.

"Because Nicolas Adams is not of age, he will remain incarcerated until we return to New Bedford in six months. Our trip must be cut short. Nicolas Adams will then be turned over to the authorities, where I expect he will hang for the death of my beloved uncle, Jeremiah McGuire. The only justice for a murder is for the murderer to die, and you, boy, will die."

"I didn't do it," I yelled. "Tell him—tell him the truth, Henry." All eyes turned on Henry, but he just looked down and said nothing. He betrayed me. I could have forgiven his silence the night before, for he had been in shock, but now, now it was unbearable, because only Henry could set the situation right.

"Take him out of my sight before I take justice into my own hands," Captain Laughlin ordered.

I ended up locked and chained in the tiny storage berth, which was filled with old rope, tin cans, tacks, and other assorted supplies. I could barely stand or breathe; I felt I would die in the darkness. Then, two days later, hope came in the form of Henry. When the door opened, he ran to me and hugged me. He brought me some bread and beans, which I greedily ate, after days of plain broth.

"My God, you look terrible."

"What's happening?" I asked.

"Well, I insisted that I be allowed to see you, and I've warned them that Father will be furious over the events that have occurred."

"You've told them, told them the truth, right?"

It took him a minute to answer. "Yes."

"So why am I still here?"

"It's more complicated than that!"

I was frustrated beyond patience.

"How could you let this happen, Henry? I told you to forget about McGuire. Why didn't you listen?"

"I couldn't allow him to hurt you anymore," he answered.

"Well, look where your actions have gotten me. What did the captain say?"

He looked down suddenly, as if he couldn't bear to look me in the eyes.

"I told him the truth," he said quietly, "but he won't accept my word. He feels I'm protecting you."

"But why, why won't he believe you?"

"He, like all the others, heard you threaten to kill the old man, and then I even went to Thompson—"

"Thompson? Oh, Henry." I felt ill.

"He influences the captain, so I tried," said Henry, tears welling in his eyes. "I have tried, but nothing is working."

"God damn you, Henry. Why won't it work? I could be put to death for this. But you, because of your father, you would be spared. They would help you. After all, it was an accident."

"I'm, I'm sorry, Nic. I tried to make amends." Henry looked away, then continued. "I'm so exhausted. And Thompson won't help, even though he knows I'm telling the truth."

"Why?"

"He's jealous of you."

"We are childhood friends. Why should that be a threat to him?"

"He doesn't want you and me to have any sort of relationship, and he's told the captain my story is false."

Henry stopped.

"Damn it, Henry, this is my life. When we get back, I'll hang. That is, if I even make it back. I can't spend months locked up in here. I swear I'll die here."

Henry was silent.

"It's a mess," he finally said. "And it's all my fault."

"You think I don't know that?" I said, my voice rising. "I know everything. I know Thompson fancies you, that you two had relations."

There, I had finally said aloud what I had only hinted at with him before.

"It's true," Henry admitted, looking down.

"You and him together, it's a sin."

"He's told me he loves me."

"How could you be with him?"

The thought of Henry and Thompson together turned my stomach. I then wondered what Henry's father would think or do if he knew what his son was doing aboard his ship? What would the people in New Bedford do if they knew?

"Why wasn't our friendship enough for you?" I asked. "Why couldn't you just control yourself?"

There was silence. Henry's dark eyes seemed to peer into mine, then suddenly the words came out like a ricochet, as if Henry knew that if he stopped, he wouldn't be able to say what he had wanted to say for a long, long time.

"Thompson will never help us because the night we fought, I told him my heart would never belong to him. Because it had always—and would always—belonged to you. It's you, Nic. It's you I've always wanted. I don't want to be with Thompson; I long to love you, to do what I do with him with you."

For just a moment I felt happy. After all, it was what a part of me also wanted. Then my reasoning interfered with my emotions.

"It can't be, Henry. It's a sin. What would everyone think?"

"I don't care," Henry said. "I don't care anymore. No one needs to know what we do. You want this too. I know you've been jealous. Don't you love me?"

Yes, I loved him; yes, I felt more connected to him than anyone. But we had always just been friends, and that's the way it had to continue. Nothing else was acceptable. I would not give in to my feelings.

"You're disgusting," I roared.

I regretted the words the second they left my mouth; I could see the searing cut they left in his saddened face. My conflicted feelings bubbled up now, and I turned away. I was afraid for my life, angry at Henry, and angry at myself.

After a minute of silence, Henry said, "Please don't say that."

I remained silent.

"Please, Nicolas."

I remained silent.

"Well, I suppose our friendship is over," Henry said, tears spilling over his dark eyelashes. Before I could answer, he turned and walked out.

I drifted in and out of a misery-laden sleep that night. I thought I would die in that closet-like jail, but that would not be my fate. Instead I was awakened by the creaking of the door. As it opened, I looked up and caught a glimpse of Thompson coming through. Two others followed, but I never saw them clearly; they were upon me too quickly, putting a gag in my mouth and a cloth bag over my head. I struggled as they tied my hands behind my back and bound my legs together.

"The captain will get his justice," Thompson whispered into my ear as they carried me out on deck. I knew then that they were going to kill me. Panic surged through my body, and I shook violently, like fall leaves do just before a strong wind rips them from a tree. Suddenly I felt myself airborne. They were tossing me overboard—my destiny, like that of so many others through the centuries, was to embrace a certain watery grave.

I went into shock as the cold water enveloped me, then struggled against my ties. Suddenly the cloth bag over my head came off, after which I was able to get out of the hastily tied ropes around my wrists and legs. But it was all for naught, because the *Mary Selina* was already moving away from me. I flailed desperately.

"Will no one help me?" I cried. "Help! Henry, help!" I realized as the words came screaming out that it was far too late.

I stopped struggling then. I allowed myself to sink, opening my mouth, choking as I disappeared down into the blackness of the waves, a searing burning in my chest.

PART II

Adrift in the Middle

CHAPTER 11

First there was nothing—only darkness.

Afterwards, I felt warm; calmness flooded my being.

Then there was light; I saw light.

Then I awoke, if you can call it that.

I was lying on a cot in what looked to be a rather sparse room—it had a wooden floor, plain white walls, a table, several almost empty bookshelves, and a few chairs that had been drawn up to a blazing fireplace. I sat up just as an older, rather odd-looking man entered the room. He was dark, stocky, and curly haired and dressed in a puffy-sleeved beige shirt, a vest, knickers, and leggings. He looked very sixteenth century. Shakespearean.

"How do you feel?" he asked.

"Wh—, wh—, where am I?" I stuttered, weakly.

"Do you remember what happened, Nicolas?"

"Who are you?" My head felt fuzzy. For a moment, I felt confused; then in a flash, it all came rushing back: Henry, the ship, being tossed overboard, my drowning. Or had I drowned?

"I don't understand. What's happened? Did you rescue me? I thought I . . . passed."

"Well, *dead* is a word for those who are still Earthbound, Nicolas. And you're not."

"What do you mean? Am I dead?" I demanded.

"On Earth you are," he said quietly. "I'm sorry."

I burst into tears then, for I was too young to be dead, and now I would never see Henry, or my mother, or New Bedford again. While I cried, the man sat quietly, staring at the fire. Finally I was done, and as I looked around at my sparse surroundings, I was flooded with doubts. None of this made any sense. If I was dead, then where was I? Was this Heaven? This wasn't what I had imagined or what my father had described to me. Where were the pearly gates? The winged angels? Where was Jesus?

"There is no way this is Heaven," I yelled at the odd stranger. "Now tell me the truth. Who are you?"

"I am Magellan, and you're in the Realm, and I can assure you that yes, this is part of Heaven. There are nine heavenly dominions, and this one is the closest to Earth, and therefore very Earth-like. As for me, well, I'm your guide."

"So, if I'm dead, and this is some sort of heavenly dominion, as you call it, then where's my father? Why isn't he here? I always expected that when I died . . ."

The words expired on my lips. Died. I still couldn't believe I was no longer alive. It took me a moment to continue. "I always believed I would see my loved ones in Heaven. My father is a good man. Why isn't he here?"

"We don't all end up in the same location at the same time, Nicolas. You will see him, eventually. But in the meantime, you've been sent here for a reason."

"By whom? Jesus?"

"God, or whatever you choose to call the powers of the universe, sent you here."

It was all too much to comprehend. "I just want to see my father," I cried.

"I promise you will, but for now, Nicolas, you need to relax, recover, and let yourself feel what you need to feel."

I was going to say something, but then a wave of exhaustion like none I had ever felt before hit me, and I collapsed back down onto the bed.

CHAPTER 12

I didn't get out of that bed until three days later. I felt drained of all energy, and a terrible feeling of sadness and anger had overcome me, so I spent the days crying, sleeping, and trying to adjust to the fact that I was indeed dead. It wasn't easy to accept, and in the face of that, nothing seemed to matter. But by the third day, I'd had enough of the sadness and anger. Dead or not, I still existed. I had to face my lot.

I rose from the bed and immediately noticed a very alive feeling. My stomach was growling. I felt hungry—an odd feeling for a dead person! I looked around the room and noticed that to the right of the bed, thick green drapes hung over a windowsill. I pulled apart the curtains and gasped. Before me lay an emerald-hued field that seemed to stretch out into infinity, and although there were no trees or bushes or flowers to embellish its plainness, the vividness and the brilliance of the green of this field had no comparison on Earth. I wanted to run outside to see more.

I turned around, flung open the door before me, and stepped out into the living area of what was a rather small cottage. No one was around, but I was immediately assailed by a most wonderful smell: fried eggs, ham, and bread. My gaze wandered over a fireplace, several wood chairs, and a shelf. Then I noticed a circular dining table next to the far wall. Generous portions of food were laid out, and after all the oversalted, sometimes rotting food that I had eaten aboard the *Mary Selina*, the temptation of this banquet was impossible to ignore. I rushed over. I sat at the table, let hunger overcome my manners, and began wolfing down the food, not caring if it was for me or not.

Before I could finish, the front door of the cottage opened up, and the odd-looking man, who had identified himself as Magellan, walked in.

"I'm sorry I didn't wait," I said, my cheeks flushing in embarrassment.

"It is fine," he said. "The meal was for you. I see you are up and with an appetite. That's good."

"I find it odd that I'm eating," I said. "My body feels the same as when I was on Earth."

"While a lot is the same, a lot is not, but you have time to learn all this, Nicolas. The transition is a great one."

"So now what? Why am I here with you?" I asked.

"This is where your life took you," he answered.

"Just my fortune," I muttered. I glanced at his face, hoping I hadn't offended him. "Look, I just don't understand," I said apologetically.

"Nicolas. It's going to take some time to comprehend everything, and some answers, just as when you were alive, you will not receive at this stage. So my advice: take the moments as they come, and the Realm will unfold itself to you when you are ready."

"Fine," I said, suddenly irritated with his vagueness. "I'll just finish my breakfast then." And I stuffed another piece of bread into my mouth.

After breakfast, Magellan took me for a tour of sorts. He called his cottage the Chalet, and on the outside it was lovely: a gray-stone structure bordered by pink rosebushes. It had been built atop a hill, and as I stood there, I felt a soft, warm breeze tickle my skin. I looked up into a sky that was bluer than any blue I'd seen on Earth, almost purple in color. It was then that I realized the intensity of colors was one of the differences between nature in the Realm and that of Earth. The clouds were whiter than white, the roses' pink hue like none I had ever seen, and as I stared into the sky, I saw a streak of bright crimson move through the sky. A flock of cardinals.

"So there are birds and animals here," I commented.

"Yes, they appear when they want to. As I told you, the Realm is quite similar to Earth in many, but not all, ways," Magellan answered as we continued our walk.

I had an urge to sketch. There was a daisy-strewn field at the bottom of the hill and a still blue pond that was exquisite. I thought of Henry, wondered what he'd think of all this if he were here. Then a great sadness struck me, and I had to hold my breath to stop myself from crying. I forced myself to concentrate on what was before me and stared more closely at my oddly dressed "guide," as he called himself.

"So, as my guide," I said, "what is your purpose?"

"To prepare you for what awaits you. But that's enough for today, Nicolas. You need to take this transition slowly, so let's head back to the Chalet. I think you'll find something you like."

My father? I thought excitedly as I ran through the front door. I was disappointed to find no one there, but a sketchbook and a set of colored pencils had been set on the table I had eaten at earlier. "Are you a mind reader too?" I asked Magellan.

"Let's just say I have intuition about you and what you need," Magellan answered.

So for the next week, I took the sketchbook and filled it with drawings, including one of Magellan that I sneakily drew one night as he was falling asleep by the fireplace.

The Realm seemed all quite wonderful, quite beautiful, quite peaceful, and I knew I had come to a good place. But it wasn't enough. I still didn't have any answers as to what my purpose was now. I didn't have my father, and there was no Henry. So the next morning, I approached Magellan.

"I want to understand why I'm here," I demanded, as we shared a breakfast of oatmeal and bacon.

"So you're ready then? Ready for more answers. You're sure?"

"Yes, I need to know."

"Well, once you know, everything gets put in motion, and your time of rest pretty much ends. Are you sure you want to move forward?"

"I think so. I mean, are we the only ones here?"

"Feeling bored with me already?" Magellan laughed.

"No, of course not," I quickly answered, not wanting to offend him again.

"No indeed, Nicolas; there are many others here, and you'll meet them eventually. But first you must meet your master. Tomorrow I'll take you to meet Leonardo. He will explain everything."

"Master?"

"You'll get your answers tomorrow," Magellan promised.

CHAPTER 13

The next morning, we traveled on foot to what Magellan called Leonardo's Woods, trekking down the hill from the back of the Chalet to where it met up with an expanse of forest. I followed Magellan onto a soft path padded with thousands of pine needles. The path was bordered on either side by trees of all types and sizes: oaks and birches, palms and evergreens. It was a stretch of green like an unending emerald river, and I felt as small as an ant at the base of a giant sequoia tree, a speck in an endless, expanding universe.

While the trees were overwhelming in size and scope, something was missing. It took me a minute to realize that there was a strange silence to these woods; I heard no chirps of birds, nor the crawling, scurrying of creatures through bushes or underbrush. Also lacking were the often earthy, sometimes pungent and raw smells of nature. These woods were visually beautiful, but somewhat sterile.

"Where is the wildlife?" I asked.

"As I told you, they come and go at their will," Magellan said. "Obviously they don't want to bless us with their presence now."

I could never have imagined such a place on Earth, and if I hadn't been following Magellan at a rather quick pace, I might have stopped to sketch the scene. What perspective would be most interesting, I wondered? On the path or off? What would make a good focus for the foreground, and how would I create the depth of the scene? My mind mulled my artist-side's thoughts until Magellan's quiet and distinct voice distracted me. "We're almost there now."

I looked ahead. The path had split into two—to the right, a trail entered a thick barrier of trees; to the left, the distinctive pine needle path continued but with fewer trees surrounding it, so that I glimpsed a view of nearby fields covered in purple flowers.

"We go left," said Magellan. "Soon you'll meet your master."

I didn't know what to make of the title. "Master." Was he God? Or a person whom I would serve? As we continued walking, I noticed what looked to be white sprinkles drifting down from the sky, and as I looked closer, they increased in amount. It was snowing. How could that be, when we had just left such warmth? I shook as a cold draft of wind overcame me, and watched with amazement as the pine-laden path, purple fields, and tree branches began changing to white.

"He's in a winter mood," Magellan said to me as we continued down the path, which was now powdery with snow and bordered by the most beautiful icicle-laden trees I'd ever seen. I wished again that I could sit down to draw the scene before me, which suddenly reminded me of New England. I thought of my parents laughing on a snowy Christmas morning, and of Henry and me throwing snowballs at each other. It made me sad, and I stopped walking for a moment.

"I see you like the ice-dressed trees," said Magellan. "They are quite lovely."

They were lovely, but as a sharp chill cut through the core of me, I realized I wasn't dressed for winter. I still wore the clothes I had worn on the ship, although they were clean and untattered now.

Magellan saw me shaking with cold. "Just think of what you require," he said. "Think of it in your head."

I looked at him as if he were insane.

"Do it. You'll see it works."

Warm. I need to be warm. I squirmed, as I suddenly felt as if a blanket had been thrown over me. A heavy, pungent wool overcoat now covered my clothes, and thick, heavy leather boots appeared on my feet. I no longer felt cold. I looked over and saw that Magellan was also now dressed appropriately, with a long, heavy cloak. It was my first, but not my last, experience with one of the special things about the Realm—its magic.

We continued heading briskly down the path and before long were knocking on the round wooden door of Leonardo's hut. I found that I was still shivering, but it wasn't due to the cold anymore. I was nervous about meeting Master Leonardo. Then the round door opened and Leonardo appeared before me. He was a small man with long white hair that had grown like a wild garden around his delicate facial features.

"So, Magellan, I see you brought Nicolas. Welcome," he said, stretching out a wrinkled hand. His handshake was surprisingly strong for someone who looked so old.

"Hello," I said, and we followed Leonardo into his abode.

"Sit down, sit down," he said, pointing at the chairs nearest the fire.

"He's ready for some answers," Magellan said.

"And so he shall get them," Leonardo answered.

CHAPTER 14

The hot tea I sipped tasted exceedingly sweet. I sat on a chair in front of Leonardo's fireplace, which was blazing with a toasty and crackling fire, and noticed that Leonardo's abode was furnished as sparsely as Magellan's was. Magellan had stepped outside and left me alone with Leonardo, who now stood over me silently, and as I looked around, I wished he would say something. I had no idea what to say to this stranger who was my "master," whatever that meant.

After a few minutes of this awkward silence, he spoke. "Well, my boy, I'm waiting. I hear you have some questions that need answering."

"Wh—, wh—, why am I here?" I asked tentatively.

"Do you mean in the Realm or here with me?"

"Both, I suppose."

"As Magellan probably explained to you before, this is where your life experiences took you. Some people end up in higher dominions of Heaven. Places you will learn about in time. But for me and you, our life experiences led us to the Realm, and when a person has recovered from the transition, as we call the time after death, there are three tracks of movement in the Realm—rebirth, play, or work. Some may be offered the opportunity to go back to Earth—to be reborn. Others get to endlessly play. Play, in this sense, is whatever a person wants it to be. There are those who sail; some travel the universe; others read and write. But you, Nicolas, have not been offered that. You are here to work."

"Figures," I said sarcastically. "I guess all the slave-like work on the ship wasn't enough, eh?"

"No, it's not that. It's just there's more for you to do and experience yet."

"More to do. I'm dead! What can I possibly do that would make a difference to anyone or anything?"

"The universe, with its many functions, needs lots of workers. Here a person might find him- or herself appointed to the Council of Judgment or the Council of Planning. There are also librarians and artists, and others who work Earth-like tasks. Some are guides like Magellan or masters like me. Masters in the Realm are leaders and teachers."

"An artist, now that would be nice," I said.

"Yes, but that's not what you've been assigned."

"So what am I to be?"

"You've been sent to become an assignment angel."

"An angel? You're jesting with me, right?" The whole idea was ridiculous. I had never really thought about angels when I was alive, but I knew my father had believed in them, sometimes quoting passages from the family Bible. "I'm no angel, Leonardo," I said, recalling my feelings for Henry.

"You were a wonderful person on Earth, and you'll continue to spread that light on Earth, just in a different form."

"'Wonderful' is an odd way to describe me. I don't think I lived long enough to be, well, wonderful."

"Others viewed you that way."

They didn't know my sinful desires, I thought.

"Angels have a special role in the universe, for they are the strongest connection between Earth and the nine heavenly dominions," continued Leonardo. "As an angel, you'll intervene in Earthly events that will put your powers to use. Your assignments will of course hinge on the powers you're granted, which are based on the skills and interests you had while you lived. On Earth, angels appear in different forms. Some look and sound just like living humans, and so a person might encounter an angel without realizing it. Other angels might just be heard, not seen; others are totally invisible in all physical ways; and some can move items or manipulate nature."

It all seemed like too much information for me. Powers? What sort of powers would I be granted when I had lived such a short, and mostly sheltered, life? I tried then to remember if I had ever come across anyone who might have been an angel, ever had an experience that had seemed otherworldly, but I came up blank. No, I hadn't encountered any angels on Earth. The closest I could think of was Henry, remembering the beauty of his face and how good I felt when he was around.

"So what if I don't want to be angel," I said, still thinking the whole idea odd.

Leonardo burst out laughing so loudly that I was somewhat taken aback.

"But Nicolas, this is what you were appointed to. You're already an angel," he said, "albeit an untrained one. You must be trained, and so you will stay with me for a while. With time, you'll see that this role fits you."

"But what about others in the Realm? When will I meet them?"

"You will meet the community here after you successfully accomplish your first angel assignment. Think of this as a sort of apprenticeship. Once you accomplish your first assignment, you will officially be one of us. But preparing for these assignments takes time and concentration, and until then, it is best you're not overwhelmed with too many new people and new things. For the next month, you'll stay here with me to train, and at the end, you'll be sent back to Earth for your first assignment. Now, let's bring Magellan back in. He must be cold."

Magellan came in all wet and red-faced. "So, Nicolas, what do you think about being an angel?" he asked me.

"I suppose it is what must be," I said quietly, really thinking it was the oddest thing ever. Powers? This was ridiculous.

"Don't worry. I'll come back to see you off for your first assignment," Magellan added.

"Come back? I thought you were staying here with me." I dreaded the idea of Magellan leaving. He was the only person I was even somewhat familiar with now, in this very alien place.

"No, I cannot stay. I must return to my chalet. But don't worry," he said, noticing the look of unease on my face. "Leonardo will be here for you. He is an excellent teacher."

"I suppose," I said disappointedly as Magellan headed back out into the cold. "You will come back, right?" I yelled after him.

"Of course," he said, walking off into the darkness.

And so I faced my otherworldly future with some trepidation.

CHAPTER 15

It was a night of troubled dreams.

"I told him my heart would never belong to him, because it had always—and would always—belonged to you."

"You're disgusting!"

Henry's shocking admission, and my cruel response, resonated in my head, waking me. In one dream, it was he who was drowning and I was trying to save him; it made no sense. After all, it hadn't been Henry who had drowned, but me, and he had been responsible. As I slowly sat up, my body felt as stiff and painful as if I had been working aboard the *Mary Selina* again, spending hours rigging lines and mopping decks with Henry.

I suddenly was angry at myself. Why was I thinking of Henry again? Just the thought of him brought stabs of sadness that cut into my core. I shook the thoughts away and forced myself up and out of the cot. This was not the time to reflect on my life. I had to concentrate on the assignment before me, because there was nothing else I could do. This was my reality now. So I went out into the front hall and found Leonardo waiting with breakfast. His breakfast table was far less extravagant than Magellan's had been. It consisted of simple toast and coffee.

"So, how did you sleep?" He peered intently into my face, as if examining me, and I wondered if he somehow knew about my nightmare.

"I'm fine," I answered, not wanting to share with him any information about Henry. I wondered then if he knew of the circumstances of my short life, of the horror of my death, of my feelings.

"So, how much do you know about me, Leonardo?" I asked, sipping on the strong coffee.

"I know that you died an unjust death. That you are a fine, rather quiet and constrained person who was cruelly drowned. I know enough about you to know that you're in the right place now," he said.

As I looked into his small gray eyes, I wondered if he knew about my secret passion and shame concerning Henry. I did not want to discuss it with him.

"What can you tell me about yourself?" I asked.

"That I am here for you now," he answered.

So he was going to be vague. Then I would continue to not be forthcoming either, I decided.

Later that morning, we walked out into his woods, and I was glad to see that they were no longer snowy, but green, and the air was fresh and comfortable, like a cool spring day.

"What happened to the cold?" I asked.

"A new day, new weather," Leonardo answered.

It was going to be a long day, I thought. I suppose Leonardo picked up on my frustration, because he quickly turned to giving me some specifics. "So let me tell you what you're training for, Nicolas," he said. "You loved the ocean, didn't you?"

"Yes," I said, suddenly picturing Henry's smiling face as he stood on the deck of the *Mary Selina* on that first day we had sailed. "It's amazing, and I learned to love it even more during my time aboard the whaler."

"It is unfortunate that your murder interrupted the tasks you might have accomplished at sea, and so that's where you will work. You will be a rescue angel for people who are lost at sea."

"Rescue angel? There are rescue angels? Why wasn't an angel sent for me? Why wasn't I saved?"

"I don't know the specifics, because our orders originate from outside the Realm, but I can tell you that angels don't always intervene. Some situations, no matter how unjust or how sad, are not part of the plan of the cycle, and it's the cycle that drives our work."

"What is the cycle?"

"The cycle is the order that drives the universe. It's what is, what isn't, what should be, and what must come to pass."

I had more questions to ask, but I held my tongue. I knew I wouldn't understand everything, and perhaps it was better that way while my emotions were still so confused. But as we continued to walk, and I thought about helping others who were stranded at sea as I had been, I felt confused. Although I liked the idea of sparing others the fear and agony I had gone through, I wondered how I, who had not been able to save my own self, would be able to come to the rescue of others.

CHAPTER 16

I sat at the shore of a flat blue lake and attempted to create waves. I stared at the water nearest the shoreline, but instead of focusing on the liquid, my mind was awash with Henry. I saw Henry's profile as he tied off lines and then turned to me and smiled, his thick black hair cascading off his forehead. He had laughed heartily at my first clumsy attempts to tie proper nautical knots, but in his dark, deep eyes, there was only affection, no malice.

"Nicolas, are you concentrating?" Leonardo barked at me. "Nothing is happening."

It was my third day with Leonardo, and I was finding the mental aspect of my training grueling. The physical part was easy. I had no problem racing through the woods or climbing up the trees; after all, I was a young man. To become this rescue angel, I needed to be a strong swimmer, which I already was, so I found the hours spent swimming in this lake near Leonardo's Woods enjoyable. I felt confident, too, because he had said that on Earth, my skills would even be stronger. But the mental part—now this was draining.

"I can't do it," I said, trying to shake the thought of Henry away.

"But remember, you did it once. Magellan told me. When you were walking to my house, when you created warm clothes for yourself during the snowfall."

He was right, but I hadn't been able to duplicate whatever I had done then, and I was becoming increasingly disheartened. It had come so naturally that day, but since then I had found my thoughts unfocused, often drifting to images and memories of Henry. Leonardo had ordered me to spend hours meditating to find a peaceful place inside of me, and to do two things: First, release the past. Second, use the power of my mind to change something, move something. "Influence change," he'd said.

Supposedly this "magic" was easily accessible to all in the Realm. For Leonardo it meant changing the weather at will, creating elaborate dinners if he did not want to spend the time cooking, and moving large stones as we walked if they impeded our path. "In the Realm we can all do this," Leonardo said. "But if you can't concentrate enough to do it here, then you won't be able to do it on Earth."

I knew my problems were related to my failure to release the past. I couldn't do that no matter how much I tried. I would tell myself that I could forget all that had happened, but then night would come, and I would dream of Henry. As I ran or climbed the trees, I'd think of New Bedford and my mother and father.

I didn't tell Leonardo about any of it, and when he asked me if I had yet come to terms with what had happened to me, I straight-out fibbed. One night we sat talking as he peeled a bunch of potatoes he was preparing as a side dish for a steak dinner. Unlike on Earth, we didn't need to have farm animals or go to market to purchase food; instead, Leonardo would concentrate on what he craved, and the food would magically appear on the table—sometimes cooked, if he wasn't in the mood to cook it himself, or sometimes, like tonight, unprepared, when he felt like cooking.

"Nicolas," he said. "You know that going back to Earth can be dangerous, especially on your first few assignments. It's the same for all new angels."

"What do you mean by dangerous? We're already dead," I said. "What else could possibly happen on Earth that's worse than that?"

"There are other things, but I just want you for now to heed these words. When you're back on Earth, don't dwell on anything related to your death. Fight the urge to return to where you came from."

"Why?" I asked.

"Because it could lead you to fall to the dark side and not be able to return to the Realm."

"But why?"

"Listen to me, Nicolas. This is important, and I'm warning you. Do not go back to New Bedford yet. Do not look for your family or other loved ones. You will see them all in time, but your assignment is just that, an assignment. Do your job, and then use your mind skills to come back to the Realm. Do you understand? Can you do that?"

"Yes."

That night I sat on my bed, peering out of the window in my room. The drapes were spread to either side of the two windowpanes, which were pushed open. I would try one more time to use the magic of the Realm to close that window. I took a deep breath and stared at the windowpanes.

Close, I thought. *Move inward. Move inward towards each other.*

I detected a slight movement, then suddenly a memory of home barged into my thoughts: Mother and Father closing all the windows in our house in New Bedford as the first roaring winds of a nor'easter blew in. The panes in front of me stopped moving. I had failed again.

I had lied to Leonardo. I couldn't do it.

CHAPTER 17

I was awake long before Leonardo came to rouse me, for this was the day I would return to Earth. I was being sent on my first assignment. Would the time element on Earth match my time in the Realm? These questions whirled in my head. About a month had passed since I'd been training with Leonardo. Like on Earth, one could follow the come and go of days with a sunrise and sunset.

Although I had struggled with the magic, slowly I had improved. Using only my mind, I had finally been able to, at times, push logs and rattle tree limbs. I had moved a fork, and yes, one day I created waves in the lake where I trained. But what I had kept from Leonardo were the many more times when he was not around and I had failed. When thoughts of Henry, of home, of my murder still haunted me, choking my attempts to master the magic. What he didn't know was how much my mind was still in the past, and I couldn't bring myself to talk to him about it because I knew it would all come to talking about Henry, and sharing my unnatural feelings towards him. I sat up suddenly, my heart pounding, wondering what it would be like to be on Earth again, especially given that I would be invisible.

Several days earlier, Leonardo had explained to me how I would appear, or rather, not appear, to those on Earth. After an hour of swimming, I had come to shore expecting, like always, to see Leonardo sitting there, but he was nowhere. I figured he must have had to go back to the cottage and decided to head back on my own. As I began my walk though, I felt something punch my shoulders forward. I turned, expecting again to see Leonardo, but again there was nothing there. It scared me, and I began walking faster, every so often turning my head to see if someone or something was coming. Then it happened again, an abrupt push.

"Who's there?" I yelled. "What are you?"

Then I heard a giggle and jumped back.

"Don't be scared; it is just me, Leonardo."

"What?"

And before I could say anything else, Leonardo materialized before me.

"I just wanted to show you how you will appear on Earth, Nicolas. I told you once that some angels appear as humans, others are totally invisible, and some can only be heard. Do you remember?"

I nodded yes.

"Well, that's how you will be. You will be invisible to sight, but not to sound. Humans will hear you, and if you touch them, they will feel you. You will be able to manipulate material things."

"But why can they not see me?"

"For a few reasons—one being that we find with sea rescue angels, invisibility seems to work best. Those lost in the middle of the ocean with no vessel or shoreline in sight do not react well to seeing a human appear out of nowhere. But the other reason is you. You just are not ready to be seen."

Again I wanted to know more, but I knew the answer would not be forthcoming, so I thought about what I did have. I would be able to interact with people, talk to them whether they believed I was there or not. That would be very interesting, to say the least.

As I recalled all of this, and the events of the last few days, I felt dizzy. I could wait no longer to rise from bed, so I got up and made my way to the front of the cottage, where I found Leonardo already up.

"I've made us an exceptional breakfast today," Leonardo bragged, pointing at the table, which was filled with various meats, muffins, and fruit. While everything looked delicious, I felt myself gag at the thought of eating anything. My stomach was churning with nervousness.

"You will have many challenges, and you need to be strong for this first assignment. So eat up," Leonardo ordered, making me sit at the table.

I ate to please him, forcing a few slices of bacon down my throat, the undercooked greasiness making me suddenly queasy. Then I reached for an orange, which I swiftly and raggedly peeled, enjoying its sweetness as I popped the seedless slices into my mouth. Then I was done. I would not eat any more.

"Let's go," said Leonardo, leading me outdoors once again.

We were to go out into his woods, as it was from there that the transfer to Earth would take place. I followed him as we walked through a thicket of oak trees, their gnarled branches creating an archway above us. We made our way until we reached a clearing that circled a clear blue pond, and standing there was Magellan. He had returned, as promised, looking as silly as ever in his sixteenth-century tights and pantaloons.

"We meet again," he said warmly, extending his hands. I grasped both of them, so happy to see him.

"I'm glad you're here to see me off," I said.

"I hear you have done well with your training. I am so proud of you. Are you ready?" he asked.

"Yes," I lied, feeling suddenly nauseous.

"You will do fine," he said confidently.

"Nicolas," Leonard said, interrupting our reunion. "I will hand you your assignment. Open it. Read it. And do like we practiced. Reflect. Then, when you find yourself back on Earth, observe and reflect. The answers will come. You will see how easy it is."

"Let's go then," I urged, suddenly impatient.

"One last thing, Nicolas," said Leonardo. "Remember my warning. Do not go to New Bedford. At least not yet. You will be tempted, but you must pass on that temptation for now."

"I won't go," I said.

"Good. Okay, here it is," he said, reaching into the white satchel that he carried over his shoulder. He pulled out a rolled parchment that was tied with gold string. It was my angel's order, and I knew that upon it would be only a name, age, and location. It would be the person I was to work with—in my case, to rescue. I rolled the string off, unrolled the scroll, and read it aloud.

"Michael Hughley, age five, Atlantic Ocean, Key West, Florida."

"Close your eyes now, Nicolas. Reflect."

I did that, repeating Michael's name, his age, his location, over and over again.

After a while, I fell into a sort of hypnotic state, almost asleep.

CHAPTER 18

When I awoke, I felt like I was still dreaming. I was back on Earth. It was dark, and the howling wind shook any complacency I might have had right out of me; I was out at sea in a storm. A whirlwind of rain and wind and water enveloped me, the waves slapping upon and over me. Though the storm was ferocious, I felt afraid for only a moment, because I quickly discovered that my skills were as advanced as those of the creatures who spend their lives in the currents. I didn't need to float, tread water, or swim to stay afloat, and if I went under, I had no limitations based on how long I could hold my breath. I was already dead anyway.

I did feel very cold, and I was surprised to realize I wasn't wearing any clothes. It didn't matter, I supposed. After all, no one would see me. But I still felt uncomfortable with my nakedness, as someone who had always been modest. So the first thing I did was meditate until I found myself wearing the same white cotton shirt and duck trousers I had worn in my days as a seaman. I had no need for shoes, at least not yet.

I suddenly remembered that I was here for an assignment. That was my priority. Although my field of view was limited, I knew that the child Michael had to be around here somewhere, so I began swimming. Leonardo's words suddenly popped into my head. "Reflect and observe. Reflect and observe."

Where are you, Michael? Michael. Michael, I thought. It was like meditating, a calm place in my mind; all the wind and water and howling seemed to disappear.

After a minute or so, I noticed what seemed to be a brown piece of wood flipping towards me, tossed by the waves. It looked to be a piece of railing from a ship. Then I spied other wreckage—glass containers, wooden chairs, tin cans—and I realized I was in the debris wall of a ship that had sunk, and that Michael had to be nearby.

I heard him before I saw him, a child's terrified wailing. I followed the sounds to see the heartbreaking scene of a near babe, alone, stretched out and holding on to a plank of wood for dear life as he sobbed. He wore a white dressing gown, like the ones I had worn as a babe, as if he had been sleeping when disaster had struck.

"Mommy, Mommy," he yelled desperately, almost losing his grip and slipping into the maelstrom as the waves pounded the plank. Within a few seconds, I was upon him.

"Michael. Michael," I whispered. "It's okay, Michael. Hold on. I will take care of you."

He was too young and too much in shock to pay my words much heed. But what I needed to do came easily to me. Treading water, I held him sturdily on the plank and whispered to him words of comfort. I eventually found myself singing a lullaby my mother had sung to me so long ago.

I was still worried I wouldn't be able to save him. He was shaking with cold, and if he didn't get warm, he would die from the elements. I pulled myself farther onto the plank, nearly flipping us over, then enveloped him in my chest. I had to get him warm, but I had nothing material to use. I began my meditation again, this time repeating the word *heat* until I finally felt my body emitting a warmth that seemed to help the boy.

He eventually fell asleep in my arms, and in the morning, when the sun rose in a spectacular array of colors, I knew I had saved his life for the moment. But he still needed to get to shore. I was thinking about dipping my legs back into the water and propelling us towards shore when, at a distance, I saw Michael's salvation. Heading towards us were two wrecking crews on longboats, come to see what riches the cruel ocean had gifted them, but also whether there were any survivors they could help.

I had heard of the wreckers who worked in coastal communities, mostly off the Florida Keys. They had existed in my lifetime, so I thought now that perhaps my time in the Realm had been somewhat parallel to the time that passed on Earth. I might still be able to find Henry, and perhaps I could . . . No. This was not the time. I shook my head and focused on Michael. The boy still slept, and I would have to wake him up, get him to make some noise so the wreckers would notice him.

"Wake up," I urged, shaking him gently. "Wake up, Michael."

"Mommy?"

I shook him a little harder. He must have become scared then, and he began crying, a piercing childish shriek. I kicked my legs hard, splashing water and hoping that between the crying and the splashing we would get the attention of the wrecking boats. Suddenly one of the crafts headed towards us. I waited until they neared and a rugged-looking crew member reached over to pull the still-shrieking Michael from my arms. I gently kissed the boy on the cheek as the wrecker pulled him away, and then I slipped back into the water and swam away.

I had accomplished my first mission, and I knew that I was supposed to go back to the Realm, but as I gazed at the ocean around me, I decided to wait. I wanted to explore more of this

Earth in my newfound state. So I dove beneath the waves, thrilled to be able to see underwater as clearly and comfortably as the fish could.

Below me lay an undersea forest of coral in a panorama of amazing colors. Yellow porous fan-like coral swayed next to tall white castle-like formations. A red garden of flowerlike plants seemed to erupt when a school of tiny yellow fish swam through and around them. I found some manta rays to swim alongside and enjoyed the exhilaration of an incredible freeness. Then I saw a pod of dolphins swimming past me, and I shot off to join them, bemused by their eternal grins. I was reminded of my time aboard the *Mary Selina* and the day Henry and I watched in amazement as two of these creatures followed in our wake for hours.

Henry. I wondered where he was, what he was doing. What was life like for him now?

Life. At least he had it. I had been cheated out of mine, all because of his betrayal. I felt an explosion of anger and floated to the surface, where I let the current carry me where it willed.

It was so unfair. How could the captain have jumped to conclusions and refused to believe Henry? How could Thompson and his thugs murder me—tossing me overboard like some leftover bones? The more I thought about it, the angrier I felt.

Then I could hear Leonardo in my head. "Observe and reflect. Observe and reflect. Observe and re—" I pushed his voice out of my head. I knew I was supposed to return to the Realm. It offered a new beginning for me; after this assignment, I would meet the other angels and maybe make new friends. But I didn't care. I had to see the three men who had led me to my death: my captain, his first mate, and my best friend—the one I had loved most in life, who at the end had become my Judas.

No, I wouldn't go back to the Realm. I would go to New Bedford. They had to pay for what they did.

CHAPTER 19

I swam and drifted and swam all the way to New Bedford, catching the Gulf Stream to aid my journey. With my enhanced abilities and the strength of the Gulf Stream current, it took me one week to do what would have taken the *Mary Selina* about five weeks of sailing. I couldn't just will myself there through meditation though. Leonardo had explained that: the only place we could travel via meditation was between Earth and the Realm. Once on Earth, even angels with our supernatural abilities were bound somewhat by Earthly physics. We had to walk to get somewhere, open doors, and so forth.

My week in the sea was splendorous and filled with colorful encounters. I stared in amazement at a school of sailfish, whose colors spun into a wave of rainbows as they herded a smaller school of fish into a circular path. I glided peacefully next to a loggerhead turtle as it made a solitary trip north. One day I spotted a sailing ship in the distance, making its way south, and my memories overtook me: Henry's dark eyes, playful and mischievous, laughing at a randy joke one of our shipmates made one night. Then that memory was overcome by a vision of those same eyes turned away, avoiding me, as I was falsely accused of murder.

The more I dwelled on that vision, the angrier I became and the faster I swam. I didn't have a plan. I just knew that I had to somehow wreak revenge for the great sin that had been laid upon me. This was my mantra, my focus, as I shot through the waves towards New Bedford, until I finally reached my destination.

I swam up through the channel to the wharf district I had left so long ago, during my short life here. At the docks, I reached out to grasp the wooden pilings, then struggled mightily to pull myself up and onto the walkway. My body felt weak, and I almost fell over as I tried to stand. When finally my legs felt grounded, I stood up and looked around. I was home, after so long. Tears sprang into my eyes as I gazed upon the cobblestone streets and red brick buildings of my old town. How I had missed it—all of it.

There were the same horse-drawn carriages and women dressed in ruffled gowns and bonnets. There were still scruffy-looking sailors milling about the square. But something . . . something had changed. There were fewer ships at the docks than I remembered, and the whole area seemed less alive, much quieter, than when I had left in 1857—a year that had seen dozens of ships go out to hunt whale. What had happened?

I wasn't sure what my plans were, but I knew I needed more information, including about how things had changed and what year it was. But first I wanted to get comfortable: my clothes were dripping wet, and my water-shriveled skin was sticky. So I meditated myself into cleanliness and clean clothing, then decided I would remain for a while at the wharf, where I had spent so much time during my life. I sauntered in and around and behind the people who made their way there every day: sailors and businessmen, families and tavern patrons.

It was my first time experiencing the odd feeling of being invisible. I could stand right behind or next to someone, and they wouldn't sense me at all. It was both good and bad. There was a certain thrill at being like some old-world spy gathering secret information, yet I felt so very alone. I wanted to join in, to feel alive, to be part of what was happening. I almost spoke a couple of times but caught myself. What would be the point? What was I to any of them?

But my silent listening served its purpose. Soon I had learned a lot about the changes that had occurred to the town and even the nation since my death. Four years had passed. It was 1861 now, and it seemed that the whaling industry was in decline. Some new substance called petroleum had been discovered and was now being used in place of whale oil. There were also substitute materials being used for whalebone. The marvelous creatures themselves were disappearing, perhaps from overhunting, and a war—yes, a war, a civil war, unimaginable to me—had led to the sinking of many whaling ships.

I was eager to find out more about what was happening in my country, but then I remembered. I hadn't come back to New Bedford for this—to find out about these Earthly happenings. I had come back for Henry, for Captain Laughlin, and for First Mate Thompson. I had come back for revenge, and I would get it.

My plan was to start with Henry. As I journeyed towards his home, through the streets I hadn't seen in so many years, I passed the Seaman's Bethel and couldn't resist stopping there. Perhaps I could find out about Thompson and Laughlin first. After all, there were always sailors young and old hanging about the place and sharing tales.

The bethel, a white wooden chapel with a towering spire, was a popular stop for the town's sailors and their families, a place to pray when disaster struck and gather to socialize for special events. It was pretty empty today. Just one sailor was inside, staring at one of the plaques on the walls that commemorated the sea dead, and an older woman was bent in prayer in the pews. I walked slowly up the main aisle and stepped up into the bow-shaped altar, which was something I had wanted to do as a child when I first snuck a peek into this very unique place of worship. Then I slowly walked around, staring at the marble plaques, some black, some white, and wondering if anyone, other than me, had died during the voyage of the *Mary Selina*. I was almost ready to leave when I noticed a black marble tablet that seemed larger than some of the others. And there I caught my breath as I read the following:

> In memoriam to the lost crew members of the *Mary Selina*, departed from these shores in 1857:
>
> Jeremiah McGuire, murdered September 28th, 1857.
>
> Cleophat Thompson, Denny Reilly, Marco Menendez, Thomas Gleig, Seth Talbot, and Hardy Simpson, crew of the hunting boat which on November 1st, 1857, was dragged away by a whale, never to be seen again.
>
> Captain Samuel Laughlin, who just hours from entering home port was felled by heart disease on May 10th, 1859.
>
> This plaque is erected here by the surviving crew.

Of the three I sought revenge on, two were already gone: Captain Laughlin, and Thompson—who had died only about a month after he murdered me.

It saddened me to think that Denny, who had always defended Henry and me, had faced the same cruel fate as someone like Thompson. You would think I'd have felt some joy on discovering Thompson's and the captain's demise, but instead I thought of myself—why was my name nowhere on this plaque? Had they somehow deemed me unworthy of being memorialized, my reputation stained as the murderer of Jeremiah McGuire, when it was Henry who had—accidentally—killed him and Thompson who had murdered me? It was so unjust, so unfair. An almost primeval anger surged in my chest. Yes, Thompson and Laughlin were dead, but Henry presumably still lived, and I set my sights on finding him.

CHAPTER 20

When I saw Henry, I almost changed my mind. There he was, walking up to his home with his mother at his side, his hands filled with a cache of papers. He was dressed like the fine gentleman he was raised to be, wearing a white linen summer sack suit and a straw hat, and he was as handsome as ever.

A part of me wanted to yell at him, berate him for his unforgivable actions aboard the *Mary Selina*. Another part of me wanted to hug him, to touch him, for my feelings for him were not so easily brushed aside by my life's painful ending. So I just stood there in a silent uproar, watching and waiting, until I noticed that Henry was not the same.

Yes, he was as handsome as ever, but the quality of his being had changed. He seemed much older than when I had last seen him. He was a young man now, no longer the teenager he had been four years ago. Yet though he had to be twenty years old, physically he seemed frailer than when I knew him. He was pale, and his dark eyes, as soulful as ever, were haunted, surrounded by dark circles. There was an air of suffering about him. I almost felt sorry for him, and for a moment, I thought that perhaps I would leave him be. Then his mother spoke.

"So she'll be here tomorrow, and we'll have the most wonderful lamb entrée for dinner."

"Yes, Mother," he said. "I know she will be pleased with your attentions, as always."

"Well, the wedding is just three months away. We are all so excited."

"Yes. I am too. She's a fine woman."

Henry was getting married! How could that be? He clearly preferred men. Was he just trying to please his family? After all, they had wanted him to marry even years earlier. Perhaps he had never really loved me. Perhaps he had wanted me only for sex, as with Thompson. I felt a cold hatred creep into me. How dare he get married and go on with his life when, through his great injustice, I was now a spirit who had left the Earth much too young? No, I would not leave him yet. I would attach myself to him and follow him, silently. I was much too angry to speak to him. But I began shadowing him that day.

The next morning, I watched as he picked at his plate of biscuits and gravy, ignoring his chattering sisters and barely responding to his mother's rant about everything that still needed to be done in preparation for Shelley's visit that night.

"Excuse me, Mother," he said, standing up from the table and heading towards the stairs, his footsteps slow and labored. Why was he walking like an old man? Was he ill? When he reached his room, he closed the door behind him, sat down on the bed, and put his head in his hands. Then he lay down, not sleeping, just staring at his bedroom wall. It was the saddest I had ever seen him. He, who had always had the advantages of wealth and looks and family position and had been filled with such energy and mischief, seemed defeated. It made him almost a stranger to me.

For a moment again, I felt my anger wavering, but then I remembered: He deserved what he was going through. Look at what he had allowed to happen to me. *At least he's alive,* I thought. *He can find happiness again.* But for me, there were no more choices. I was dead and assigned to be an angel whether I wanted it or not. To hell with him. Let him suffer.

There was a knock on his bedroom door.

"Henry!" his father yelled. "What are you doing in there? I need to see you."

"What do you want?" Henry responded.

"Meet me downstairs in the library," his father ordered. I followed him down to where Mr. Lawton waited, a pile of papers in his hands. "This is the quarterly financial report from Mathison," he said, handing Henry the papers. "I received it yesterday. Read it."

"Can this not wait, Father? It's Saturday, for goodness sake." He set the stack down.

"No, it cannot. I am worried, son. Our profits have dropped nearly five percent again. We must do something to change this. Surely there is something that can be done, and we need to start addressing the problem now."

"Damn it, Father, today is Shelley's dinner, and I am tired of hearing you complain about our family fortune. I told you to invest with Mr. James, invest in the petroleum, but no, you could not imagine things would change. And now you expect miracles to save us."

"If our other business investments do not turn around, Henry, your inheritance will not be what you expect. How will your pretty little fiancée feel then?"

"If she wants to marry me for the money, then good riddance to her," Henry boomed.

He left his father standing there and headed straight to the kitchen, where his mother was giving orders to the cook and staff. And that was how I spent most of the day—watching Henry and his mother oversee staff as they cleaned the house and prepared the supper. Finally, as it came to half past four in the afternoon, Henry excused himself and went upstairs to bathe and dress. Two servants came up and laid out a large piece of oilcloth upon his bedroom floor; then they returned with the empty bath basin and took turns filling it with warm water.

I watched as Henry undressed and slipped into the water. *He is way too thin,* I thought, remembering the lean muscles I saw so many times aboard the *Mary Selina*. I couldn't help but enjoy seeing him, however; he was still all I could want. Then I realized that in a way, this was perverse. I wouldn't like to think that a spirit had watched me in my most intimate moments.

But as Henry got out of the tub, he turned his back to me, and I almost screamed. His shoulders and back were criss-crossed with scars. My God, what had happened to him? When? Was it on the *Mary Selina*? Had Thompson done this? Had he been punished for something after I died? I couldn't imagine the captain would have allowed anyone to do that to the ship owner's son. Or had his father been abusive, beaten him barbarically? That had never been my impression of Mr. Lawton, and I had known him since childhood. I didn't know what to think.

After Henry dried himself off, he dressed in a starched white shirt with a black tailcoat, a low-cut white vest, and a bow tie. As he combed his dark hair, I thought he looked stunning. Too thin or not, he was still to me the most beautiful creature I had ever seen. I wondered suddenly if Leonardo and Magellan knew where I was and what I was doing. Could they read my thoughts? Did they know the shame of my attraction to Henry and the depth of my rage against him?

I didn't have much time to dwell on these worries because Henry left the room. I followed close behind.

As he made his way down the stairwell, I caught sight of a young woman speaking with Henry's parents. A pretty girl she was, fair-haired and blue-eyed, soft-spoken, and polite. Her dark blue dinner dress accented her coloring nicely. I didn't recognize her, but then Henry's youngest sister Louisa ran up to her.

"Shelley, I'm so glad you're here," she said.

Wait. Could it be? Oh my—yes it was. It was Shelley Witham, from so long ago. The girl Henry's parents had wanted for him all along, the one they believed was a good match for their son. The girl we had planned to play a joke on. The girl he had not really been interested in because, as he had finally admitted to me, he loved me. So this was who Henry was engaged to.

I stopped as Henry proceeded down the steps to greet her affectionately, kissing her hand as she blushed. I felt a twinge of jealousy, but not as much as I had expected. Shelley could have passed for my sister if I had one, and in a way that gave me some comfort. Perhaps Henry had not totally forgotten me. Standing together, they looked the perfect couple. To someone who did not know what I knew about Henry.

A half hour later, Shelley and Henry's family sat on bench seats around a candlelit dining table for a rich supper that included soup, roast mutton, currant jelly, stewed fruit, and vegetables. I stood behind them.

Shelley and Henry enthusiastically discussed their upcoming nuptials. It would be the social wedding of the season, for both the Lawtons and the Withams held high positions in the community. But I wondered. Henry had been attracted to men. Had that changed? If not, his marriage would be a farce. Did his engagement weigh on him?

Mr. Lawton lifted a goblet in cheer.

"To my son and his lovely fiancée, and to a new beginning and life for both."

Then he turned to Shelley. "I will always be grateful, my dear, for you coming into Henry's life again, just when he needed it most, after that ill-fated cruise in which so many men were lost. It has made all the difference."

"I love him very much, sir," was her response.

"So do I," I whispered angrily, regretting immediately that I had spoken aloud. Shelley seemed to have heard. She looked around in confusion.

"What is it, my dear?" Mr. Lawton asked.

"Nothing," she said. "I thought I heard something."

My powers of whispering were real. I could be heard.

Later that night, I followed Henry and Shelley as they took an evening stroll along the wharf. My heart ached as they held hands, wishing it were mine he touched. At one point, Henry turned to her and kissed her. Why could I not be the one who felt his lips? How I wanted to hold him, press my body against his. Feel his chest and thighs against mine. That would never happen now.

But no, I shook my feelings away as I had when I was alive. It was wrong, and truly, what was I now? A God-awful shade, a ghost. I didn't feel angelic. I had rebelled against all of Leonardo's instructions. I looked around me, suddenly wondering if Leonardo would come or send someone to retrieve me, and then what. Would I be sent away from the Realm? Where would I go? To Hell? Surely if there were nine heavenly realms, there'd have to be at least one Hell. I wished that I had asked Leonardo about that. I felt ill then, nauseous with fear and emotion, and I ran from those I had followed, taking the long way back to Henry's house to wait for his return.

When he finally returned and turned in to his bed for the night, I could not stand the silence. As he lay back upon his pillow, I spoke, in what I knew to Henry sounded like a whisper. "How could you?" I hissed. "How could you?"

He jumped from his pillow, looking from side to side, his eyes wide with fear. It was then I realized how I would get my revenge.

CHAPTER 21

A month passed. My haunting of Henry intensified. Each day, and only once a day—for better effect—I would whisper something to scare and upset him. Sometimes he would sit with Shelley on the bench on the front porch, and I would whisper, "Murderer, murderer, murderer," until he could stand it no longer and would run to his room, saying he had a headache. At other times, I would hiss, "How could you?" into his ear as he held her hand. "Liar," I would call him on other occasions.

My whispering wrought its vengeance, with Henry breaking down in private tearful moments and sleepless nights. Henry did not share his torment with anyone, not even Shelley. I think he thought he was going insane. Perhaps this was what insanity truly was—a person haunted by a dark spirit.

Eventually my haunting left its visage on every pore of his being. The dark circles under his eyes were even more pronounced. His face was paler, vampire-like, and his thinness started to look sickly. Still, the plans for his upcoming wedding continued, uninterrupted. The household was busy and seemingly joyous with preparations, as it had been decided that the wedding would take place in the Lawton manor.

His mother and sisters especially enjoyed it when Shelley and her mother came over to plan final details. I couldn't stand being around any of them and would flee the room immediately, the sight of Shelley too painful. She was getting what I so wanted. Still, there was some joy in knowing that my whispers would leave her with only a shell of the man I had known.

Then, four days before the nuptials were to take place, Henry finally seemed to break. Usually fashionable and neat, he showed up at his job in an unkempt state—with an unwashed face, dirty shirt, and no vest. His father was appalled and immediately ordered him home to clean up. Instead of going upstairs to wash, as I had expected, Henry headed straight to the family library and rolled aside the two bookshelves that shielded the entry to our secret room—the room where we had enjoyed so much of our childhood.

I followed him in. The room looked the same as when I had been there years earlier. There was still the same large wooden sea chest and the decorative shelf filled with scrimshaw figurines. Except now in one corner was a safe, which I imagined held some of the family's most expensive jewelry. Suddenly a host of life memories came to me—of Henry and me playing games, plotting jokes, and dreaming of our future. When I looked at Henry again, he looked frantic—his face red, hair messy. Then he spoke—to me.

"I can stand this no longer. Either I am insane, Nic, or you are actually here. Damn it! I know you're here. I've heard you; I've sensed you—for the past month. I have tried to ignore you." He took a breath. "What do you want from me?" he yelled. "I cannot change what happened."

I would not give him the satisfaction. I would remain silent. But he just stood there, with his sorrowful dark eyes, and finally I could stand it no longer. "Your suffering," I whispered.

He stumbled back sharply, as if he'd been shot. "Yes, I know," he finally answered. "I deserve that."

Then I noticed that tears were running down his cheeks. "I don't expect you to forgive me, Nic. I cannot forgive myself. Do you want to see what I have to do to get by? Do you know how hard it is for me to go on, knowing what happened to you, because of me? I was and still am a coward. Why do you think I agreed to marry a woman I do not love, at least not as I loved you? I thought I could do what was expected of me, but now . . . Look, Nicolas. This is what I do, when my memories of you cannot be locked away anymore, when I cannot forget what I caused to happen to you." He began unbuttoning his dirty white shirt, then stripped it off.

I was shocked again at seeing the mess of his back, and now I knew it was self-inflicted.

"I know I should not be here," Henry said. "I should have been the one they killed that day."

He went to the chest and opened it up and pulled out a cat-o'-nine-tails, like the one Thompson had used aboard the *Mary Selina*. Then I watched as he beat himself, groaning in pain, until he opened up the scars into a fresh and bloody mess.

"Stop it!" I exclaimed, horrified.

"There, is this enough suffering, Nic?" he groaned.

I did not answer. He sat down on one of the settees and turned his face to the corner where I stood. I realized that he sensed where I was even if he could not see me, even if I did not whisper.

"I've thought a lot these past few weeks," Henry said. "Thought about what a great injustice was done to you, and how I was responsible for it. I loved you, Nic. God knows I loved you—even when I failed you. Now I believe there is only one way to right this wrong. You will like this," he said, pulling open the sea chest and reaching in for something.

I caught a glint of silver as he pulled out his father's pistol. "Perhaps with my death, Nicolas, I can gain your forgiveness and you may have peace," he said quietly. Before I could react in any way, Henry stood up, put the gun to his temple, and pulled the trigger. First there was the shock of the gunshot, then the blood, and then his body fell in front of me—his beautiful dark eyes wide and staring. I thought I would see him then, a spirit like me, but no. Where was he? Why was he not here before me?

I could not move. It was not until hours later that Henry's father discovered him and began sobbing. "My son, my son," he cried, and then Henry's mother and sisters ran in and joined in the chaos. I realized then, with horror, what my thirst for revenge had wrought. The Lawtons had always been kind and fair to me, and this is what I had done to all of them. I even felt even sorry for Shelley, for I had ruined what for her could have been the happiest day of her life.

And Henry. His death had brought me no peace, no joy. What had I done to him, the person I loved most? As I thought this, I felt myself turning inward, almost shrinking. I felt myself disappearing. Like a slow-burning ember, I grew silent, extinguished by the aura of darkness and negativity that consumed me.

CHAPTER 22

Time passed . . . passed . . . passed. I was trapped, where I deserved to be and would be evermore, in the secret room behind Henry's family's library.

Eventually I stopped seeing and hearing the comings and goings of Henry's family. I never tried to interact with them, because I could not stand the guilt of what I had done. Eventually I knew his parents must have died and his sisters married and left. Perhaps none of his sisters could bear living in that house full of Henry's horrible suicide and my dark presence. Other families came and went, through many decades, but I mostly ignored them. Still, I knew that some who lived in the old Lawton house could feel my presence. There were children who would stare wide-eyed in fear at the corner I inhabited; others would cry and run out of the room. One woman became so fearful of the house that she moved her family out within the month. One family had the secret room sealed up. I don't know what part of me they felt or saw, because I had gone silent.

So time moved on and on, and I was just a part of the darkness of a universe I didn't deserve, nor cared to be part of. Then one day, I heard loud roaring, crashing, booming sounds, and suddenly the walls splintered around me and my darkness that had lingered in the hidden room for so many years was thrown into light.

Whiteness, the light of day, momentarily blinded me. Then I saw a tree. Green grass. Blue skies. The walls of Henry's old home were shattered; the house was being demolished by some sort of large, unrecognizable contraption. What was happening? The images were too much, and I had dwelled in darkness for so very, very long. I was afraid, confused, and then, in all the panic, came one simple thought, one simple name: Magellan.

I thought of him. I focused on him over and over again. *Magellan, Magellan, Magellan.* And suddenly I felt myself rising, moving, finally leaving New Bedford behind.

PART III

Afloat at the End

CHAPTER 23

Too bright. Too bright. Everything was too bright! The light seared my unaccustomed eyes. I found myself curled up on the floor in a corner of a room that seemed vaguely familiar. I squinted until my eyes started adjusting. Finally I began to figure out where I was. Before me was a roaring fireplace—its hearth cozily decorated with small statues of birds and bunnies. I was back at Magellan's Chalet, in the front room. Back at the place I had first ended up when I drowned.

Before I could contemplate the situation any further, in he walked, and after all these years, he was just the same, still wearing his silly sixteenth-century garb. I didn't know what to say. He did.

"So you've returned to us, Nicolas. I had wondered if you ever would. I feared you would be lost forever. Some are."

"Some?"

"Yes, others like you."

"Like me?"

"Yes, other angels who fall."

So that's what had happened to me. I felt ashamed and said nothing for a long while, with Magellan standing over me, watching. Finally I asked him what I feared knowing.

"Now what? What happens to fallen angels?"

"Whatever you make of it."

"God, not with the vagueness again!" I yelled. "Why can't you just give me a straight answer?"

"Do not raise your voice at me, boy," Magellan said in a strangely calm tone. "Yes, it's hard to accept, but you, Nicolas, became a fallen angel, and you must deal with it. Remember, Leonardo warned you about returning to New Bedford. About dwelling on your past. But you didn't pay heed, did you?"

I shook my head.

"Well, no matter. I'm just relieved you're back. It doesn't look good for us guides when we lose someone. The masters are never blamed; it's us guides who are looked at as being at fault. Perhaps I sent you forward to Leonardo too quickly. Perhaps you weren't ready to train yet. Perhaps—"

"Please stop. It was my own doing, and it led to such horrors," I said, flinching as images of Henry's final act invaded my thoughts.

"I know. We know what happened."

"Did you see everything? Everything I did?" *Everything I felt?* I thought.

"No, we lost you for a long while. But the case of Henry Lawton and his suicide was taken up by some here in the Realm. It was then that your presence was detected and reported to Leonardo, who of course contacted me. But as a fallen angel, it was up to you to return to us. Which you initiated when you reached out to me."

"Then you've seen Henry," I blurted out. "Is he here?"

"I don't know."

"Will the masters know? You must help me find him. I must make amends for what I did," I said, jumping up.

Magellan grabbed both of my arms and forcibly sat me down.

"Nicolas, Nicolas. You are not in a place yet to ask about Henry, let alone see him. Even if he is here, which I do not know. You've just returned to the Realm. You were fallen for so long; you need to do some work and some reflection before you move forward to anything or anyone."

"Please," I cried. "Take me to Leonardo."

"No," Magellan barked. "No. Not until you're ready."

So that was how it was; I was forced to accept Magellan's directions. As desperate as I was to find Henry, I eventually accepted that I had no choice. In the Realm, things would work, as Magellan reminded me, how they had to work. Even if Henry was only at the bottom of the hill, I wouldn't be able to see him unless they allowed it. It was useless to argue. I would have to follow Magellan's instructions.

The next morning, I arose to find myself alone. The dining room table had been sparsely set for me to eat a lone, cold breakfast of milk and plain bread. There, next to my cup of milk, was a note. I picked it up to read a list of chores:

> After breakfast trim the hedges behind the chalet.
>
> After lunch trim the hedges in front of the chalet.
>
> Then go down the hill to cut and gather logs for the fireplace.
>
> After dinner sweep the chalet entirely, then dust the tables and shelves.

I grudgingly followed the instructions and, exhausted, went to bed without seeing Magellan. The next morning, I awoke and found that I was alone again, and another note sat near my bowl of oatmeal.

> *Go to the well at the bottom of the hill and bring up five pails of water.*
>
> *Water the flower bushes that border the chalet.*
>
> *Paint the wooden door at the back of the chalet.*
>
> *Scrub out the basin in the bathroom.*
>
> *Wash the dirty clothes that are in the bin.*
>
> *Hang them to dry on the line in the back.*

I closed my eyes. More work. More orders. This surely was a punishment of sorts. I wanted to rip the list into shreds. Why was I wasting time on endless chores when I should be searching for Henry? I almost walked out then, but a thought stayed me. Maybe I had to do this. Maybe this was my last chance. What if I failed and was expelled from the Realm? Would I be sent to Hell? The thought frightened me beyond all reason.

In my short life, I had been good at following orders: my father's, my captain's, my more experienced shipmates, but this last time, when I had blatantly disregarded Leonardo, my actions had led to Henry's dreadful demise. I decided I would follow this annoying list of orders.

On the third day, I encountered a list twice as long. It seemed I would be working almost every minute of every day, and into the evening.

This went on for ten days. Still, I persevered, even when some of the work became repetitive. By the end of the eleventh day, the chalet looked spotless. Good enough for a king. Then, on the twelfth morning, as I dragged my weary body to the dining table, expecting another long list, I was surprised to see nothing there. I spun around, just in time to see Magellan walk into the room with a large smile on his face.

"Good. You've proven to us that you *can* follow orders. This is one step towards restoring your position in the Realm. Come. Let's go for a walk."

I stepped outside and once again stared up into the bluest of skies. We walked in silence, trudging down the hill and out towards a patch of sunflowers that spread out to the horizon in what seemed to be an endless green field. I felt sure that somewhere, perhaps even in the Realm, Henry was looking at the same sort of natural beauty.

"So what's next?" I asked quietly.

"You need to do more work."

"More? Why can't you just take me to Leonardo?"

No answer.

"You must take me to Leonardo," I said loudly. "I'll do whatever you ask, whatever endless list of chores again, but I insist on seeing Leonardo."

"Your insistence won't work," Magellan said calmly.

"But surely you know that I must have hope that I will see Henry again. That I will be able to apologize for what I did to him. If not, then I don't care. Perhaps the darkness is where I belong."

"Never say that!" Magellan bellowed, displaying a sudden fierceness that surprised and scared me. "What you say is a travesty, boy. I won't work with you if you feel that way. You've been given a second chance—that some never get—and you dare speak like this." He turned away from me and walked briskly back towards the Chalet. I followed him.

"I'm sorry, I'm so sorry," I said, breaking into sobs.

"My boy," he said. He ran back to me suddenly and threw his arms around me.

After I was calm, he said, "Look, I cannot tell you for sure, but I believe you will reunite with Henry, if only because your journey has been so intertwined. But for now I have some news I think you might be interested in. The work I mentioned a few minutes ago is different from what you've been doing. I'll show you back at the Chalet."

Once in the cottage, Magellan went to a bookshelf and pulled out a blue-covered book. "Here," he said, handing it to me. "This is for you."

I opened it and was surprised to find it filled with blank white pages. "What's this for?" I asked.

"Do you remember how Leonardo told you that you would meet the community at the Realm if you accomplished your first assignment?"

"Yes," I said, suddenly remembering those words from so long ago.

"Well, you did accomplish your first assignment; you did save the child, in spite of that awful detour at the end."

"I had forgotten about that," I said, recalling now the poor frightened child I had comforted in an angry sea.

"Well, because of your success with that, it has been decided that you can meet some of the others who live and work in the Realm. But first you must accomplish this one last task."

"What am I supposed to do?" I asked, staring down at the book.

"You must write your tome for Leonardo."

"What do you mean?"

"You must reflect on your life and on your fall in this journal. It will be delivered to him, and he will read it and decide if you are ready to meet the others and ready to work again. Will you do this? It is important that you go back to work. Everyone in the Realm must work, or they can't stay here."

"Yes, I'll do it," I answered nervously.

CHAPTER 24

A few nights later, I sat at the table in my room, staring at my words and wondering if I should state how I really felt. So far the tome had been relatively easy to write—my and Henry's childhood adventures in New Bedford and our teenage escapades aboard the *Mary Selina*. But now I had reached the time Henry had started his sexual relations with Thompson and I had finally realized I had romantic feelings for Henry. How could I tell Leonardo that I found Henry incredibly beautiful and wanted to kiss him, to fall into his arms? This was the Realm, after all, and, well, my feelings were still a sin. What would happen if they knew?

I looked around the room in frustration and saw the colored pencil set that Magellan had given me so long ago. Instinctively I went to it, and instead of writing words, I began drawing images. They did not lie, but they weren't a confession either. I drew a picture of Henry the night he had come in all disheveled after a night of drinking with Thompson. Instead of writing about the feeling of Henry's body against mine when we hugged, I drew him holding my hand when I was sick. Instead of drawing a picture of us kissing the way I had dreamed of, I drew a picture of Henry and Shelley together. It was the most I could give to Leonardo. It would have to do.

"Here it is," I finally said one morning, handing the book to Magellan, my hand shaking in fear that it wouldn't be enough.

"Are you okay?" Magellan asked me as he walked over to a wooden chest. From the chest, he pulled out some plain brown paper and ribbon. He glanced over at me as he wrapped the book and bound it in the green ribbon.

"Yes," I lied. "I'm just glad to be done with it."

"I will get a courier to deliver this to Leonardo," he said. "Don't worry. This is for his eyes only. It will be he who decides the next step."

"I just hope he likes it."

"I'm sure you did fine," he reassured me.

The next few days were torture. I volunteered for any chore just to fill my time and get my mind off the knot of nerves in my stomach. I expected that Leonardo would read through my ruse and know that I had not lied, but I had omitted some necessary details.

"Awaken, boy, awaken," Magellan said one morning. I sat up, startled from a deep slumber. "We got word."

"What is it?" I asked, desperate to know what the answer was one way or the other.

"It's good. Today you gather your belongings. We're off."

"What?" I said.

"I have good news for you. Leonardo accepted your tome. He wants to meet with you, but first I will introduce you to the larger society here in the Realm."

"Wonderful," I said. I would finally meet others in the Realm.

CHAPTER 25

Magellan and I sat comfortably in a horse-drawn carriage. At the front, controlling the reins, was, surprising at least to me, a young woman with a boyishly short hairstyle. She was dressed oddly too, in thick blue trousers and a heavy wool top. As I stared at her, Magellan spoke.

"Are you ready?" he asked me.

"I think."

"Do you have any questions for me?"

"Will I see Henry now?"

"I told you, I have no idea."

"All right then," I said, disappointed.

"Surely you must have other questions," Magellan pushed.

"Of course," I said. "Am I now a full-fledged angel? And what about my fall? Does that not matter anymore?"

"It will always matter, and should always matter to you," Magellan said. "You need to see that it never happens again. But don't dwell on that. Think of all the opportunities that await you. As a 'full-fledged angel,' as you call it, you will be part of a community. You will work with others and finally really be part of the Realm."

I sat back, fidgeting in my seat, my pulse racing with both nervousness and excitement. Who would I meet? What would I do? And most importantly, would I find Henry in the Realm? Even though the stay at Magellan's Chalet had been good for me, I was tired of the isolation of my afterlife. I so wanted to see what else was out there.

The trip took several hours, through mostly crisp, green, grassy fields sometimes dotted with the most beautiful purple cornflowers, golden tickseed, magenta corn cockles, and bright red and yellow poppies. In the distance, I could see huts, small homes and cabins, fences, and clotheslines. It reminded me of the outskirts of New Bedford.

Then, farther ahead, I saw the outlines of great buildings rising high into the sky. We were heading towards a city! In my short life, I had never been to a great city, but I had seen portraits of the cityscapes of London and Paris, and from a distance, this city of the Realm reminded me of those portraits from so long ago. I imagined it would be filled with horse-drawn carriages and crowds of pedestrians. It would be noisy, perhaps dirty and smelly.

About a half hour later, we drew into the city. I caught my breath. This was unlike any city I could have imagined. There were many large buildings of marbled stone, Gothic style, with towers so high they seemed to stretch up through the clouds into higher dominions. It was like a city of cathedrals, awe-inspiring, and quite beautiful of course.

But it wasn't just the look of the place that caught my attention. The city was busy. The walkways around the buildings were packed with many citizens of all ages, races, and sizes, all moving quickly towards whatever purposes they had. Also, the manner of dress varied among the many inhabitants. Some were dressed in togas and long gowns. Others were clothed like the people I knew during my days in New Bedford. But there were some manners of dress I found shocking and inappropriate. There were people whose legs were all exposed in short skirts and knickers, showing more skin than would have been allowed when I was living on Earth. There were women whose blouses seemed a little too low-cut and boys wearing low-hung or too-tight pants.

I suppose Magellan noticed the expression on my face. "I thought you would have figured out already, from seeing me and Leonardo," he said, "that here in the Realm, we wear clothes from the time period we lived in. I've always found it to be one of the quirks that make this place so interesting, this mix of humanity from different time periods. You might make a friend who saw Shakespeare live on stage and another who watched men land on the moon for the first time on television."

"Tele-what? A man on the moon?"

Magellan laughed. "Nicolas, Nicolas, you have been gone for so very long in Earth time."

"For how long?" I asked, suddenly realizing that I had no real sense of how many years had passed since I'd seen Henry die.

"It has been over a hundred and fifty Earth years, Nicolas."

I was dumbstruck. I had been trapped in darkness for that long? Henry had been dead that long? How could we ever be reunited now?

"But don't worry," Magellan said. "That's part of the reason we've come to the city. We have wonderful libraries here, and some of your time will be spent catching up on history, or, in your case, the future you missed while you were fallen."

"So what happens here in this city?"

"In many ways, it's very Earth-like," Magellan explained. "There are innkeepers and cooks, artists and architects, librarians and gardeners, and almost all other manner of trade from Earth. Except up here, we have no need for armies, police, or other careers that deal with the more unsavory aspects of life on Earth. Everything here is geared towards the angel assignments. Our dominion, like the others, is here to help carry out the master plan of the universe."

"And what is that?" I asked.

"Oh, that's a question for someone way above my position. I have no idea."

Well, my questions about the universe might have to wait for an answer, but there was one question I would keep asking until I had an answer: where was Henry? Unfortunately, Magellan was as clueless about Henry as he was about the universe's grand plan. I would continue my search on my own. I decided I would ask everyone I met if they knew someone named Henry Lawton. I knew I would probably fail in my search. There would be thousands of people with Henry's name, from many different time periods. But I had to do something. I would persist.

"But I do know your *master's* plan, Nicolas, and that is that you'll eventually be going back to work, and you need to be aware of how the Earth has evolved. I will take you to a library to learn all that, as well as to some different places to meet people so you can become a part of our community. As I mentioned earlier, angels are often teamed together for assignments, so it's good for you to make some friends. We'll be staying at an inn in the city, but first I have arranged for you to dine with a small group of angels who, like you, are young—in the sense that they too died early during their Earth journey."

"So soon?" I asked, suddenly feeling nauseous. It had been so long since I'd been around others who could see me, other than Magellan and Leonardo.

"Yes, it's time you meet others. Not everyone here is old like me and Leonardo," Magellan said wryly.

The carriage suddenly turned right down a road that was especially breathtaking. It was bordered by tall, shady oak trees to the right, and on the left was an immense sparkling azure lake. I thought we were on a cul-de-sac that, as the road twisted around, would send us heading back in the direction we'd come from, but I was wrong. From a break in the trees, a narrow dirt road met up with the street we were on. Our driver turned down that road, and ahead was a building. It looked like a barn, a plain wood structure with a flat red roof, nothing like the fancy structures I had just seen in the city.

"We're almost to the tavern," said Magellan.

The inside of the tavern was more inviting than its outside. At one end was a roaring fireplace, near a stage where four young musicians played what seemed to be medieval ballads. The smell of roasted chicken and potatoes further awoke my senses, making me realize just how hungry I was. The place was filled with large round wooden tables, all of which were empty but one.

"Your new friends," said Magellan, turning away.

"Where are you going?" I said, realizing he was leaving me here. "I don't know these people. I can't just walk up to them."

"Of course you can. They're expecting you."

"Please, it's been a while."

Magellan sighed. "I'll introduce you, but after that you're on your own. I'll be outside when you're ready to leave. It will be fine."

The situation was so awkward. I followed Magellan up to the table, where twelve others sat. I could barely look into their faces as he introduced me. When I did look, I saw two young guys who seemed to be my age, whispering as they looked me over. The girl next to them stared stoically at me. I wondered how much they knew about me. Did they know I had fallen? Had that happened to any of them? What were they thinking?

It was hard for me to focus, and I don't think I even paid attention as Magellan recited their names. I think one was named Andrew, another Steven. There was a Jorge and a Kirsten, a Din and a Mustafa, but I couldn't recall what name went with whom, and some of the names I didn't recall at all.

By the time I sat down, Magellan had already slipped away. Soon a short, husky man with a lanky assistant showed up carrying plates of food, and I escaped by stuffing my face.

At first I thought no one was really interested in getting to know me. After all, they all seemed to know each other. I glanced at a long-haired fellow to my right who was busy in conversation with two others. The girl across from me, dressed in a toga, seemed self-absorbed and barely registered any interest when she caught me staring at her. But then I glanced over to the girl who sat left of me. She was very striking—with brown, honey-tinged skin and long, wild hair that, instead of making her look unkempt, resembled that of some ancient Egyptian goddess—wild and magnificent. I knew she couldn't have died too long before, for she was dressed in trousers and a long shirt, something women in my time would not have worn.

I learned her name was Serene, and she was an eager conversationalist. By the end of the dinner, I had found out a lot about her. She had died at sixteen, like me, and she told me how she had lived with two other girls in the city, and how even though she'd been an angel for two years now, she had mixed feelings about the whole thing.

"It's got its advantages and disadvantages," she said. "If you know what I mean." I didn't have enough angel experience yet to understand what she was trying to tell me, so I didn't answer. She told me she wrote poetry, some of which she would be reading aloud tonight. Like me, she loved nature, especially trees. She made me laugh when she made fun of Magellan's outfits and the hose he wore on his stick-like legs. "I think it's time for Magellan to upgrade his wardrobe," she said. "But he's not the only one who could use a makeover. Most of the guides and masters look like total nerds."

I didn't know what *nerd* meant, but I laughed anyway. Before dinner had ended, I asked her about Henry.

"Hmm. Henry Lawton. Nope. Never met or heard of him. Who is he?"

"My best friend. I need to find him," I said, disappointed.

"Well, I'll ask around. Perhaps I can help."

After the dinner ended and the musicians had left the stage, Serene stood up. She went to the stage and read several poems, including this one, which stood out in my mind.

> *A color like mine*
> *is not to be found on a city street where colors*
>   *are used for walls, and bricks, and pain.*
> *A color*
> *like yours*
> *cannot be found in nature's paths*
> *where colors appear in sunlight or rain, on*
>   *mountain or sea.*
>
> *For true colors are only revealed*
> *when everything transforms to what it should*
>   *be.*

What was I transforming to, I thought, and where, oh where was Henry?

CHAPTER 26

Soon after that first night in the city, my life became more ordered, in a way that reminded me of my school days. Magellan and I were residing in a small apartment in the city. As he had explained earlier, it was time for me to learn about all I had missed in my fallen state. So each day after breakfast, he would take me to what he called "the Grand Library of the Realm." It was located only a few blocks from where we were staying, and when I first saw it, I believed it was far from grand. There it stood, among all the spiraling towers of the cathedral-like buildings: a simple one-story red brick building that I discovered was much larger on the inside than it seemed on the outside.

I first entered the large lobby area to find workers—the librarians—sitting behind tables. They looked to be busy staring at square black objects that I couldn't identify. One was talking to a visitor. Other than Magellan and me, however, there were few other people here; there seemed to be more workers than visitors. To the right of the librarians' tables were a series of separate marked corridors to choose from, and on that first day, Magellan led me down one marked Earth

Historical Archives. I entered a room filled with books and things called film clips and videos.

So began my research and reading. I would read books, newspapers, and magazines, look at pictures, and watch videos—so amazing. I started from the year of my death and worked my way up until the present. Although some might have found this a chore, I didn't. I was amazed at the scope of history: the inventions, the wars, the changing architecture, the leaders, tyrants, saints, and heroes. Some of Earth's history had been so barbaric in scope that I was appalled and wondered why there had been no heavenly intervention against such things. How could the Holocaust and all the bloodshed of World War II have happened? Or the atomic bombs and the random civilian bombings of modern times?

I was shocked, and glad I had not lived in the present time. Modern weaponry and technology scared me. But not all technology bothered me. Some of it was so amazingly magical, like all the medical advances that made life healthier for people, and all the tasks that could be accomplished via the boxes called computers.

Sometimes I would leave the library with my head spinning with questions, and then Magellan would pick me up in a carriage, and we would drive out of the city to the countryside. Magellan would bring along paints and easels and sketchbooks for me. He knew that it was only through painting that I could really relax. One day I found an amazing tree to sketch. It had a bright green trunk and snow white leaves, and near its top was a branch lined with a series of birds' nests. I had never seen anything like it.

And so the weeks went by, and finally I was caught up in my trek through history. "Now what?" I asked Magellan.

"You're one step closer. Now you need to reconnect with some of the people here. I know all these weeks we've kind of kept to ourselves, but that will change now. I've arranged for you to spend some time with Serene again, and she will introduce you to others."

Serene introduced me to two of her best friends. One was a dark-haired, rather plump girl named Allison, Allie for short, who seemed to be in her early twenties and dressed as if she had lived in the mid-twentieth century, in puffed-out skirts and two-toned saddle shoes. Allie seemed sweet and quiet, quite different from Serene, and I wondered how they had become friends.

Serene's other best friend was a young man named Lucio, who dressed in low-cut, baggy slacks. Lucio had short dark hair and dark eyes and classic Roman features. "When did you get here?" I asked him.

"The late 1990s," he answered.

Lucio had been an artist of some sort during his life, and our love of art was something we had in common. It led to a day for the four of us at the Realm's art museum. One of the sections of the museum, called Earth's Epochs, had displays that represented each of the Earth's time periods, and now I could see how the art—mostly paintings and sculptures—had been inspired by and reflected the time period in which it was created.

For example, there was a heart-wrenching Civil War–themed painting of a mother crying as her son, who looked only about sixteen, rode off to join his regiment. A plaque next to the painting explained that an angel who had lived through the Civil War had created the piece.

I wondered then, would I have an opportunity to display something here, perhaps a painting of one of my whaling adventures with Henry?

"Lucio," I asked. "Is any of your work displayed here?"

"I don't do that anymore," he said. "I haven't touched a brush since I've been here."

"Why?" I asked.

"I don't know. Everything is just so different now," he answered. "When I got here, I told myself that the artistic side of me was done. I didn't want to dwell on the past, and I thought that if I continued to create art, I would."

"Do you miss it?"

"Sometimes," he said. I could tell by his voice that, like me, something terrible must have happened to him. But I didn't want to impose. After all, in the Realm, people only shared the details of their death if they wanted to. Serene had told me she died in an automobile accident, and I had no idea what had happened to Allison. Magellan, like me, had drowned, but his drowning was accidental.

The afternoon at the art gallery continued in a pleasant way. Sometimes we went into a hall together; other times we went our separate ways. It was during one of those separate moments that I happened to wander into the hall on the 1940s and '50s era of Earth. As I looked around, I caught sight of Allie—who had stopped in front of a large painting of a scene depicting World War II soldiers. As I got closer to her, I noticed that she was crying. I held back, but she must have felt my presence, because she quickly wiped her tears away and turned to face me.

"Are you all right?" I asked.

"Sort of," she said quietly. I noticed then how her voice had a flute-like quality to it, very musical sounding. "It's just, what I call a death regret moment. They wash over you sometimes, you know."

"What do you mean?"

"Well, a death regret moment for me is wishing I'd said something different to someone I loved before my death. But no matter, you probably don't understand."

I didn't answer her. But of course I, of all people, knew. I with my burning regrets about Henry.

CHAPTER 27

The next day, Lucio, Serene, and I were picnicking by the lake, near the tavern where I had first met Serene, when Allison ran up to us. "I wanted to see you guys before I left," she said. "I'm being sent on assignment, and I don't know when I'll return."

"Is it badass?" Serene asked.

"It involves an elderly woman who was just widowed," Allison said.

"Sounds boring," said Serene.

"Come on, Serene," said Lucio. "All types of people need our help. Not every assignment has to involve hipsters, musicians, and hot guys."

"Yeah, but they sure do make our work more fun," she said, smirking at him.

"Don't let any council members hear you talk like that, or you might be sent away for reflection. Maybe you'll accompany Nicolas and Magellan back to the Chalet," he said, laughing.

"Oh, I almost forgot to tell you," Allison interjected. "There's some big stink going on down at the Council Hall."

"What do you mean?" Lucio asked.

"After I received my orders, I walked past a room where a group of council members were talking quite heatedly about some situation on Earth. They were talking loudly, which you know is rare in the Council Hall. So I sort of stopped outside the room, out of sight of course, and listened."

"What's happening?" Serene asked.

"I couldn't hear everything, but it involves some angels who've been trapped on Earth by a live human."

"How can that be?" Lucio asked. "That doesn't make sense."

"I don't know—that's all I heard, because someone came into the hallway I stood in, and I didn't want to get caught listening, so I left. But I've got to go get ready for my assignment. We'll catch up when I get back."

"Good luck," said Serene.

We watched Allison as she walked away.

"Wow. I wonder what that's all about," Lucio said. "Trapped angels. I've never heard of such a thing."

CHAPTER 28

Within a week, we would all know. In a most surprising announcement, at breakfast one morning, Magellan told me I was going back to work. Yes. I was going to be placed on assignment again. Frankly, I was shocked that it had come so quickly. "But first you have to meet with Leonardo," Magellan said.

I was nervous, for I hadn't seen Leonardo since my return, and I knew that I had failed him by falling, and he must have been really disappointed in me.

He was in a winter mood again, for when we traveled to his woods, again they were white with snow, and again I found myself shaking with cold and worry.

"It'll be okay," Magellan said quietly.

Leonardo greeted us and brought us into his hut. Once we were seated, he addressed the matter at hand—my assignment. He told me that three teams were being assembled to work on this one very important assignment, and he had been asked to put together one of the teams.

"I'm sure you've heard about it," he said. "It seems that everyone in the Realm is talking about this situation. You know, the one involving the trapped angels. I've put you on the team I assembled."

I was shocked. Why would he choose me for such an important task? Me—who had failed so miserably after my last assignment. I couldn't keep silent.

"I'm sorry, Master, but I don't understand why you would send me on this task. You know what I did."

"Magellan, can you step out for a moment? I'd like to talk to Nicolas alone."

"Yes, of course," Magellan said, leaving us.

"I won't lie to you, Nicolas," Leonardo said. "There was quite a bit of discussion among the masters concerning placing you on a team. Frankly, I had my doubts too, but then I went with what I've always done. I put together the team I thought would work best."

"I, I hope you won't be sorry," I stammered, feeling ashamed and looking away from his intense stare. "I am sorry, Master; I know I let you down."

"Why didn't you listen, Nicolas? I warned you."

"I couldn't be on Earth and not see Henry. It was just too hard for me. I know what I did was terrible. I don't know if I even deserve to be back here in the Realm."

"Of course you belong here, Nicolas. You're an angel. But I am concerned about you. Are you more at peace now, or do you still think of Henry all the time?"

I thought about it. My heart still ached terribly for Henry, but I also found that during these last few weeks in the city, I was able to be distracted and I'd not focused on him as much. "I think I'm better," I answered.

He stared me in the face, as if trying to read my thoughts. "I hope you're telling the truth, because as I looked at the blend of angels that would work best for the different elements of this assignment, I came up with three of you. Do you want to know who they are?"

"Yes, of course."

"They're your friends, Nicolas. It's Serene and Lucio."

So I would work with Lucio and Serene. Well, that was good news.

"That's wonderful," I said.

"Yes, the three of you together seem to have the traits and skills that will work well for this situation," Leonardo continued. "I examined each of your tomes, and—"

"They had to write tomes too?" I interrupted. "I thought it was only me, because I had fallen."

"No, every angel has to at some point reflect in words upon his or her journey."

I noticed then that my tome, in the book with the plain blue cover, lay on a coffee table in the room. Near it were two other tome books. One was decorated with elements of nature—colorful autumn leaves, twigs, moss, and ferns. I guessed that must be Serene's tome. Then I realized that the other book must be Lucio's. His cover made it look like a medieval knight's manual, with intricate drawings of warriors on horses and heralds carrying banners, and words that seemed to be Latin. I guessed that they had also to do with knights. *Interesting,* I thought.

"Do you think the pain that still strikes you at times concerning Henry will distract you from doing what needs to be done now?" Leonardo suddenly asked me. "While on your new assignment, you must focus on the work at hand. You must forget about what happened in your last assignment. Do you think you can do that?"

"Yes," I said. "I want to work again."

And I did. Not only because it was the only way I would be able to stay in the Realm, but because it would prove that I had deserved the second chance the masters had given me. Then I thought it was important that Leonardo know this.

"I don't want to go back to the darkness," I said.

"I know that," he said.

CHAPTER 29

So there we sat, the next day, all three teams, being feted at a Council celebration. This event, a rarity in the Realm, was meant to show everyone just how important this assignment was and how much support we had. Normally when an angel was assigned to a job on Earth, he or she was sent off with little fanfare, like I had been, but of course nothing about this assignment was normal.

It still surprised me that I was part of one of the groups that would be sent. We had not yet been told many details of the work, and as I looked over at the members of the other two teams, I realized I had no idea what they would be doing either. As I sat there, though, I noticed that most of the eyes in the hall seemed to be focused on our team, and on me in particular. We sat with Leonardo, the two other masters, and their teams, at a long silver table that had been placed on a platform so that we were higher than everyone else in the room.

I was so uncomfortable that I could barely sip the delicious pear nectar that filled my goblet, and while Lucio and Serene seemed to enjoy their entrée, I barely picked at the grapes on my plate. As I peered over at those attending the event, I thought I could read their expressions in the way they seemed to whisper, glance slyly at us, and then quickly look away. I didn't like what I imagined they were thinking. I was sure their thoughts were negative:

Is Leonardo crazy for putting Nicolas on the team?

Why choose him when the rest of us have never fallen?

A few minutes later, my thoughts were confirmed when a red-haired heavy-set angel walked up to me, leaned into my face, and whispered, "You are a most abominable choice. You had better not fail us."

Before I could answer, Leonardo was at my side, and he lifted his hand to quiet me. "Ignore him," he said.

But it was hard to ignore such sentiments. It made sense that others would feel that way. I looked over at the table where the council members sat. The Council of Judgment, of which Leonardo was a member, was composed of the twenty master angels who were the leaders of the Realm. I had never formally talked to any of them except Leonardo, although I had once seen Magellan chatting with several and on another day had seen a group of them walking along the city sidewalk. I wondered what they would do and say if I failed again.

Why would the angel council send me on this assignment, when there were such other outstanding angels in the Realm? During the last few weeks, I had met some of them, like Terrance, who had died a hero on Earth, jumping on a grenade so the others in his patrol unit would live. Here in the Realm, Serene told me, he still offered to counsel people who couldn't move past their sadness or fear about dying. And the more I learned about Serene and Lucio, the more I thought they were outstanding. Serene had told me that Lucio was known throughout the Realm for his consistency: he had never failed an assignment.

"He's pretty amazing," she said. "Most of us have assignments that just don't work out for one reason or another."

"Has that happened to you?"

"Yes, I've failed two of mine. I think I just didn't have enough time on Earth, enough life experience, to figure out what to do. It's a bad feeling when that happens."

Yes, I thought to myself, *it is a bad feeling.* But my failure was worse. I had fallen. Sitting at this dinner, I wondered again about the masters' decisions. Could it be that sometimes they didn't get it right?

I looked over at Serene and Lucio, wondering what they were thinking. Lucio seemed happy, excitedly talking to Leonardo, while Serene looked . . . rather un-serene, frowning as she stared across the room. "Boy, they need to liven this up," she said. "I wish they'd talk to me about how to throw a party. Where's the music?"

Lucio laughed. "Well, it's not quite like Earth, is it?"

"I suppose." She sighed. "Sometimes I miss Earth, and this party, if you want to call it that, reminds me that even here in the Realm, not everything is perfect."

I had to smile at her truth. If I couldn't make amends to Henry, nothing would ever be perfect for me.

Hours later, the feast ended, and as everyone gathered to go, we three stood outside waiting for Leonardo to say his goodbyes. Finally he was ready.

"You won't be going back to your homes tonight," he said as he walked up to us. "You'll stay with me until you leave for Earth, which won't occur until you discuss any concerns or questions you have about each other. You will not be successful at your task unless you do this. So tomorrow I will lead you out into my woods, where you will spend some time alone with each other."

"But Master, it's the assignment I'm worried about," said Serene. "You need to be straight with us. Tell us more."

"Now, Serene, I have sent you off on other assignments, and the protocol remains the same. We will speak further about this when the time is right, which is not now. What is it that I always say to you before you leave for Earth?"

"Observe, reflect, and the answers will come," we all chanted together in rote. Even after all this time, I still remembered those orders from my only assignment.

"Yes, that's all. That's all I can say now too, other than that it will be up to you to reach this human and get the angel stones back."

Well, that was a little more information. Angel stones were involved. What were they? I had never heard of them. "Angel stones?" Serene asked. "What about angel—"

"I told you," Leonardo interrupted. "Not now."

"Oh crap," Serene whispered to Lucio.

"Serene!" Leonardo admonished.

"I'm sorry," she said.

Later that night, I found myself slipping in and out of sleep, twisting and turning on the narrow cot I lay on in Leonardo's abode. What would happen if we failed? Would I be held responsible for the failure? Would I be sent away?

CHAPTER 30

The next morning, I was up early with Serene and Lucio, eating the simple breakfast of toast and milk that Leonardo had laid out for us. Afterwards, we followed Leonardo into his woods. Once again the majesty of the trees struck me. I guess the others felt it too, because Serene began reciting a poem about trees that included these lines:

> *Beauty will come to them*
> *In the rainbow—*
> *The sunlight—*
> *And the lilac-haunted rain*

"Ah, Serene," Leonardo said. "Your words are always a pleasant interlude."

"Yeah, that's cool," said Lucio. "Is it one of yours?"

"Oh no," she answered, laughing. "You should know my style by now. That's an early twentieth-century poem called 'Trees Need Not Walk the Earth' by a poet named David Rosenthal."

As I watched how Serene looked at Lucio, I wondered. Were they more than just friends? I thought Lucio and Serene would make a handsome couple. Allie had told me that here in the lowest of all the angelic realms, romance was a possibility because we were at the level closest to Earth. It was the higher angels, such as archangels, cherubs, and above, that had moved beyond such emotional and physical yearnings.

"This is where I leave you now," said Leonardo, staring at me again.

Among all the lush and blanketing trees that surrounded us, Leonardo stopped under a tree that was rather sparse and shabby, but it had a soft carpet of green moss beneath it.

"It's a plum tree," said Serene, answering my questioning look. "Knowing Leonardo, I think it's a subtle message. Plum trees represent endurance and overcoming difficulties. I guess in his own way he's letting us know that this will not be easy."

"What do you mean?" I asked.

Serene and Lucio just looked at each other. Lucio motioned all of us to sit, which we did, but then we sat silently and awkwardly until he spoke up. "So, when you came back, did you have to see anyone else first before you went to Magellan's?" he asked.

"No, straight to Magellan's," I said.

"I've wanted to say this to you for a while, Nicolas. I didn't want you to think strangely of me, but now seems the time," Lucio said. "You look like I'd always imagined angels to look like when I was alive. If I had known you then, I would have painted you."

I smiled at him, thinking his comment ridiculous and wondering why he was delaying the conversation about what he really wanted to talk about.

"What do I look like, a cherub?" I joked.

"Have you ever seen one?" Serene suddenly interjected. "I've always wanted to."

"No," I answered.

"Ah, cherubs, the beautiful puppies. That's what I call them," said Lucio. "No, Nic, you don't look like a cherub, but there's something about you, with your long fair hair and your light eyes, that reminds me of the angels in medieval paintings."

"Yes, your eyes are very ethereal," Serene added. "You are the most typically angelic looking of the three of us."

"That may be," I said, and laughed. "But I am the worst of all."

Lucio and Serene glanced at each other as if acknowledging a prior conversation, then stared back at me.

"So you've seen cherubs?" I asked, hoping to get their minds off of me.

"I have," answered Lucio.

"So you visited one of the higher realms? What was it like?" I asked.

"Look, guy, I might as well just lay this out," Lucio said. "We're here to talk about you. Serene and I need to understand what happened to you on your last assignment. We're not here to judge you, but if we're going to work successfully as a team, we need to trust each other. Serene and I don't know your story, other than that you . . . fell. Leonardo felt it was best that the details come from you."

"I don't know if I can talk about it," I said, feeling as if I were about to drown again. Although my life with Henry was always on my mind, the thought of having to share aloud with Serene and Lucio how horribly it had ended seemed particularly painful. How could they, who were so successful as angels, ever understand what had happened? And how could they understand my desire for Henry?

"There's something I want you to know, Nic," Serene said. "I was weak on my first assignment. I almost fell, and that was one of my failures."

I looked into her dark eyes and believed she was telling me the truth, but I knew she was only telling me this to make me feel better, which was useless.

"That may be true, but you *didn't* fall," I replied. "I am the first fallen angel that either of you have ever met. Isn't that true?"

"You shouldn't continue to call yourself that, Nic. Yes, you fell, but you rose again."

"I don't understand why. The masters won't explain anything."

"That part hasn't played out yet," Lucio said soothingly. "But we've been put together to try to save two angels who are trapped, and we need to stay focused on that matter."

"Then let's do that," I said angrily. "Why do you need to know my past?"

"Because it matters. Serene and I may need your help down there, and we need reassurances that you're not going to fall again. A team cannot be a team without trust, and I won't work with you if I can't trust you."

"Okay. Okay," I said, exasperated with his insistence. "Fine."

So I told them most of my story—leaving out my romantic urges—up until the point when I first saw Henry again, but then I stopped. I couldn't take myself there. I felt as if I would break, both physically and mentally, if I told them about the darkness. They looked at me, their eyes urging me to go on with my story.

"What happened with Henry?" Serene asked.

"I got my revenge," was all I could say. We sat there for a few moments, they expecting more of an explanation, and I unwilling to give it. Finally Lucio realized I wasn't ready. Not ready to speak the total truth that I had excluded from my tome.

"Let's go back then," Lucio said angrily, rising. We followed him silently back towards Leonardo's hut. I didn't care that he was angry. I didn't want him knowing the depth of my sinful feelings and actions.

CHAPTER 31

Later that afternoon, I sat at a rather tiny peach-colored table, uncomfortably close to a fuming Leonardo. He had sent Serene and Lucio off on errands and had called me into the sitting area. I could see the disappointment in his tired-looking eyes and a tenseness in the corners of his mouth.

"Explain yourself, young man. You told them most of the story. Why couldn't you share the ending, like you did with me in the tome?"

"I just couldn't," I said. *If only you knew I didn't tell you everything either,* I thought.

"I had hoped that the writing exercise would have helped in your healing, in your ability to exhume the past, but I see I was wrong. You're still not ready. Perhaps I should not have convinced the others you were ready to go back on assignment. I should have—"

I interrupted him with a plea.

"No, I am ready, Leonardo. I'm ready to work. I want to stay here, and I know that involves work."

"But your team members—they must trust you, and to do that they must know what happened on your last assignment.

Serene seems satisfied with what you told her. She feels she knows enough, but Lucio isn't sure."

"So it's up to them?"

"Yes."

"If I can convince Lucio, will you let me be part of the team?"

"Of course."

"Let me talk to him then," I said.

So Lucio and I went back into the woods, back to the same plum tree we had been at early in the day. I knew this would be my last chance to stay on the team, so I made my earnest plea. "I know I didn't tell you everything, but one day I will."

Lucio just looked at me. "What are you afraid of? You've already shared the story with Leonardo."

"I don't know. I just can't talk about it with you yet. For now, can't what I've told you be enough? It's enough for Serene. What do you think of me?"

"You're someone who had a great injustice done. But I worry that that injustice left you weak, prey to emotions that might affect our team now. You're a question mark to me. I want to know what you did to Henry and why you made that choice. Otherwise, how do I know you're not going to fuck this up for us?"

"That won't happen, Lucio. I promise. You have no idea how much I fear falling again. I would never risk it, I swear."

"Can you try to forget about Henry while we're on assignment?"

"Yes," I lied.

"Ah," he muttered. "I just don't know. It's not just about you. I'm good at what I do, Nic. I've experienced a success here in the Realm that I never had on Earth. It's the one thing I like about being dead. You know my reputation here. I've never failed in an assignment, and I don't want you screwing it up."

Before he could finish, up walked Serene, snapping away the tenseness like a fresh wind in a stale room.

"Hello," she said. "So you two made your peace?"

"There's no peace to be made, Serene. It's about trust. Can we work with him? Is he ready?"

"Lucio, let's give him a chance."

I wanted to hug her then.

"Why should we?" he asked.

"I trust him. Don't you trust my instincts?" she said, reaching for his hand. The look in their eyes was one of warmth and intimacy, and I knew then that yes, they must have shared a romance.

"Of course," he said. "I trust you."

"Well then, let's tell Leonardo that it's okay with us," she said.

"Fine," he muttered. "Fine. But if something goes wrong, I won't forgive either of you, and it's on you, Serene."

It was then I realized for the first time the power a beautiful woman might have over a man.

We stood up to head back, and when I glanced upward, I gasped. Our plum tree had changed. We were now sitting under a taller, thicker-branched, full-size tree.

"That's cool," said Lucio. "What's that about?"

"It's a linden," said Serene, noticing it too. "Lindens are trees that are known as village guardians. They represent peace and justice—which is up our alley, eh?" she added, a big smile spreading across her lovely face.

CHAPTER 32

I expected that we would be briefed and then sent on our assignment the next day, but I was wrong. Leonardo said we had to meet with a special visitor, who would explain all the details of our assignment. We were ordered to rest and relax until he came.

"Special guest? What's that about?" Serene asked. "No one in the Realm ever gets referred to as a special guest."

"He must be from one of the higher dominions then," said Lucio.

My curiosity was piqued. While our realm, the lowest, nearest Earth, was just called the Realm, the eight others had lyrical-sounding names: Unirea, Nefrosti, Irelae, Venufri, Edanom, Raraia, Salastari, and Eathelum. I wondered which one our special guest was from.

The following morning, I took my sketchbook into Leonardo's Woods, but before I could decide what to draw, Lucio and Serene showed up.

"This is a good spot," Lucio said. "That tree's a good choice for your drawing."

"You never did tell me what type of art you did," I said.

"I started off as a street artist—graffiti."

"You mean *scribblings on walls*?" I asked.

"You might look at it that way, but graffiti has been around forever, although maybe it's not always been called that. I don't think it was as common during the nineteenth century either, so you might not be that familiar with it," Lucio answered. "Like I said, that's how I started, but eventually I put my work on canvas."

"What were your paintings like?" I asked.

"All fantasy. You know, dragons, gnomes, knights, things like that. As a teenager, I enjoyed those types of stories." So that explained the cover of his tome.

"I'd like to see your work," I said.

"If it's possible when we go to Earth, if we have time, I'll take you to see the only permanent pieces I did, which ended up at a children's museum."

"That's impressive," I said. "Your work ended up in a museum?"

"Well, it was more a matter of circumstance than perhaps my talent, but . . . I don't want to get into all that now. We need to head back; Leonardo asked me to come and find you."

"Any news?"

"That's what I think he has for us," Serene said. As we neared Leonardo's abode, we were shocked to find it was no longer a hut. Instead of the two-room shack, there stood a grand manor complete with an iron-gated entrance, lush, colorful gardens, and a separate carriage house.

"That's kicking awesome," said Serene, her jaw dropping open.

"You know how things work here," said Lucio with a smile.

He was of course right. In the Realm, anything could change, depending on the circumstance or mood. Obviously this guest was important; thus Leonardo had willed his regular living quarters into something more regal. Now in front of us stood a stately brick manor surrounded by gardens.

"Ah, on time," said Leonardo, walking down the entrance path. "Do you like it?

"Of course," said Lucio.

"Our guest deserves even more, but as a simple man, this is the most I could muster," he said, winking at us.

We walked into the front room, which now was like a medieval great room decorated with red and gold velvet-lined chairs and huge tapestries that immediately caught Lucio's attention. He had said his artwork had focused on fantasy and medieval themes, and the tapestries had wonderful images, such as knights on horseback, castles on hills, and unicorns in forests.

"Master Leonardo, these are amazing," Lucio said.

"I knew you would like them, Lucio, but if Serene and Nicolas look, I think they'll find something for them too."

I moved from tapestry to tapestry until I found what he was referring to, and lo and behold, there on the bottom right of one of the grand tapestries was a rendering of a great whale and sailing ship. A few minutes later, Serene yelled out.

"Oh, I see it. Look, here's for me," she said, pointing to a block that contained renderings of some of Serene's favorite writers and poets. Shakespeare, Wordsworth, Austen, and one I didn't recognize. "That's Toni Morrison," she explained.

Then, after a few minutes, Leonardo bid us all to sit. The lighting in the room seemed to have changed; it was brighter than it had been minutes before. We looked at each other silently, then saw a most marvelous sight—one I will never forget, for our special visitor was indeed quite special, emitting an effulgence like I had never before seen.

CHAPTER 33

It was Gabriel! Even angels don't necessarily get to meet Gabriel, or for that matter any of the archangels, and yet here he was, talking to our team. This just reinforced to me how important our assignment was.

One day in the city, I'd overheard a couple of other angels talking about the archangels, and one had mentioned how Gabriel sometimes appeared in the feminine form of Gabrielle. That seemed odd to me. Anyway, to us he appeared as Gabriel: a tall, muscular, dark-haired man, an incredibly beautiful being who spoke softly and eloquently. He emitted a great aura, light blue in color, that spun around him like a corona around the moon. We were awed, and Leonardo had to goad us into asking questions about our assignment while we sat there tongue-tied and overwhelmed. Finally Lucio rose from his seat and spoke, very quietly.

"Sir, we are honored to be in your presence."

"You may sit," he said to Lucio. "Leonardo invited me here today because I was summoned by the masters of the Realm several weeks ago for advice on this situation that is unfolding on Earth. Since then I have been watching and reporting on the situation to the union of archangels on Irelae."

"Sir, if I may ask, why don't they just send you to resolve this?" Lucio asked. "Why us?"

"Because this is a problem from the Realm, involving angels of the Realm. The solution needs to arise from the same place."

He paused, then continued. "But as I'm doing with the other two teams, I will give you some background information that should help you. Do you know what angel stones are?"

I, of course, had never heard of such a thing.

"Yeah," answered Serene. "On Earth some people call them worry stones. My mom used to carry one whenever we traveled. They're usually clear stones with an imprint of an angel inside of them," she continued, talking mostly to me, who she correctly figured out wouldn't know. "Each angel stone represents a different aspect of the human experience, such as travel or serenity or love or hope. Humans pray with them or sometimes just meditate, or rub them to clear their thoughts and bring positive energy to themselves. When I was alive, I thought people who believed in those things were superstitious, but now I know better."

"Yes, Serene," said Gabriel. "There are more to the stones than most people know. The stones carry properties that are transmitted from us to the human stone makers. These human stone makers have a special connection to our kind, a power we have imbued into them on a small scale. The properties in the stones, whether it be healing or protection or some other element, can work for those humans who meditate or pray with belief, but the stones' powers are limited and depend on the strength of a human's belief. There is, though, one type of stone that has much more potency and is rarely used on Earth. These are called power stones. Power stones carry the essence of an angel and that angel's specific strengths. Every angel that has ever been created or appointed has a power stone. They are stored with the archangels—in Irelae."

"So you're saying we each have a power stone?" asked Lucio. "Why don't we know more about this?"

"Because it is unlikely you will ever be asked to use your power stone on Earth. They are used in rare cases, and only when they are asked to do so do angels find out about the stones. There is much risk when an angel takes a power stone to Earth. It endangers the angel if he or she should lose or not be able to retrieve the stone. The essence of the angel is tied to the stone, and once a human possesses the stone, that human can entrap the angel. But even worse, that human will have access to the angel's powers without limit. Throughout Earth's history, power stones have been taken to Earth only twenty-five times. One of those times was with me, long, long ago. But that's a story for another time."

"So what does this have to do with our assignment?" Serene asked.

"About a month ago, five power stones were stolen, and although they were stolen with the best of intent, the actions have been catastrophic, and the angel who stole them has now fallen."

I shivered at the word *fallen.* Gabriel peered intently over at me, and his aura warmed and overwhelmed me so much that I had to close my eyes for a moment.

"This angel," he said, "whose name is Jared, was a team leader for a group of angels sent to a South Florida hospital in the United States to help five children who were dying of leukemia."

"Wait a minute, I think I met him once. He's really tall, right?" Lucio asked.

"Well," continued Gabriel, ignoring the question, "the strength of one of Jared's team members was healing, and when Jared became too attached to the ill child he was assigned to, he demanded that the other angel heal his child too. That angel of course could not do that, and Jared became very angry. Through his master, he contacted me to ask permission to go to Irelae to discuss the mission. I gave him permission, but on the day we were to meet, he never showed up. Only later was it discovered that while in Irelae, he had stolen the power stones of every angel on his team, including his own."

"Why?" Lucio asked.

At the time, we believed he wanted to use the power of the stones to change the outcome of his assignment. But now we know differently."

"What strengths do the stolen stones have?" Lucio asked.

"They are Youth, Persuasion, Health, Bravery, and Longevity. When we discovered the theft, we immediately summoned the team back to the Realm, but by then two of the team members had already been trapped by a live person, a Julian Miller, who somehow ended up with two of the stones. Then Jared disappeared with the three other stones, including his own."

"So why is he doing this? What's the end game here?" Lucio asked.

"We don't know yet, and that's what we've sent the other two teams to explore. But your job has nothing to do with that. We want you to free the trapped angels."

"What about the other two, the angels who came back?" asked Serene. "Jared still has their stones."

"For now they're safe here in the Realm, but they cannot be sent to Earth again, cannot ever work again, until their stones are retrieved, for if a human gets their stones while they're on Earth, they too will be entrapped. As for Jared, we cannot locate him. We feel that the power of the stones he holds, including his own, are helping him hide his aura from us, as well as giving him other powers. The entrapment of angels is of course unacceptable; it has caused many aberrations to occur in the great cycle. Many things are not as they should be, and worse yet, this live human who holds the stones has increasingly used the power of the stones for evil actions."

"Well, maybe when we get near this person who has the stones, we can find Jared," said Lucio.

"No. Your assignment is not Jared," Gabriel said sharply. "Heed my words. Do not interfere with him in any way. Your assignment is to retrieve the two stones from Julian. It is the only way to release and rescue the two trapped angels. And one thing is important to remember. You cannot forcibly remove the stones from a human. The stones must be given to you of free will."

Serene and I glanced at each other. This was going to be more difficult than we expected.

"Are you sure we're the best team for this?" I suddenly blurted out. I caught sight of Lucio glaring at me.

"You should know that Master Leonardo would not have chosen hastily, for your skills, your passions, and your experiences will all be vital to the success of this mission. It is very important. Now. Sit back and close your eyes. I want you to see what is at stake."

We did as requested. An image appeared in my head, then, of two figures. They lay on the floor of what seemed a very ordinary sleeping room, with a large iron-framed bed and a simple dresser with four drawers. I could not make out any details of the figures' features; they were like gray outlines of people. Then I heard them—moaning. The moaning continued until it became unbearable, a never-ending caterwaul. I wanted the vision to end, but it continued until the vision became me—I was that pain, trapped again in Henry's house, lost in the endless, eternal darkness. Then suddenly I was out of the darkness and in the water, sinking, choking, sputtering. *How could you, Henry? How could you?*

Everything went dark.

When I awoke, I was lying on a bed in a large chamber. Leonardo sat near me on a chair.

"Oh good, you've returned to us," he said kindly. "I was worried. What happened?"

I said nothing. I was afraid to tell him that I had gone from seeing an image of the trapped angels to reliving my own hell. It would prove to him that I wasn't totally focused on this assignment, but still thinking of Henry.

"What happened?" he repeated.

I had to tell him something. I decided I would not lie to him, but just leave out the details. "I'm not sure. It was just overwhelming to see angels in that condition."

"Are you up to continuing now? If not, I'll ask Gabriel to return tomorrow."

"No. Just give me a moment. Tell the others I'll join them soon."

"Okay," said Leonardo, looking at me worriedly as he got up to leave.

When he walked out, I realized a horrible truth: my inability to resolve my feelings towards Henry might interfere with the mission after all.

Later that day, we sat again in the great room, with Gabriel before us. I had returned pretending everything was fine, and now after a nice meal, followed by an after-dinner walk, the time had come for Gabriel to leave. He was sending us off with a few last words of wisdom. With a voice that sounded like the clear bells of a cathedral, Gabriel stated this:

"Belief. Faith. Confidence. Hope. I bestow these to you."

"'Hope' is the thing with feathers that perches in the soul," Serene suddenly said. "That's what Emily Dickinson wrote."

I opened my eyes, shocked by Serene's interruption and wondering what Gabriel's reaction would be.

"Yes, I know," Gabriel said, a radiant smile lighting his face.

Gabriel then lifted his right hand towards us, as if blessing us in a way, and I felt a soothing warmth fill my being. I bowed my head, and by the time I looked up, he was gone.

CHAPTER 34

The next day, we walked with Master Leonardo through his woods. He walked at a leisurely pace, too slow for us younger entities, who kept halting our steps so we wouldn't leave him behind. The anticipation of returning to Earth gnawed at my very being, both drawing and repelling me. I was enthralled with the thought of finally getting a chance to explore an Earth that was now over 150 years into the future from what I knew. When I had finally escaped my fall, when Henry's house was destroyed, I had had no time to experience what was around me.

So what was life like now? What would it be like to actually be in one of those modern, crowded, overbuilt cities? I knew experiencing it in person would be totally different from reading about it and seeing it on film.

My excitement at finding the answers to those questions, however, was tempered by a strong fear of returning. The last time I was sent on assignment, it had ended disastrously. What if something went wrong again? What if I should fall again? What would the masters do? How many chances would an angel get?

Such questions weighed heavily on me as we walked, until we suddenly came upon a clearing in the woods. In the center was a pristine patch of snowdrop flowers; near them stood an ibis and a tall, thick tree that reminded me of an umbrella, with its canopy of branches and leaves high in the air. I had never seen such a tree.

"Wow," said Serene. Then, answering my curious look, "That's a baobab tree. In Africa they're revered as the tree of life. They symbolize endurance."

"How can you remember the names of all these trees?" I asked.

"I learned them during my life because of my interest in nature, and trees in particular. You know that's my skill, Nic. On Earth, I can manipulate nature."

I realized then that I didn't know what Lucio's skills were.

"Here's the spot," Leonardo said, interrupting my thoughts. He pointed to the large blanket underneath the tree. "Please sit."

We did as ordered.

"I know you will succeed. Because of his experience, I'm assigning Lucio as the team leader. Heed his orders."

"This won't be easy; maybe impossible," Serene whispered to Lucio. I knew that Leonardo had heard every word, just as I had, but he misunderstood Serene's joking.

"You're right, Serene," he said, verifying my thoughts. "But the greatest glory, both on Earth and in the Realm, comes from accomplishing difficult, seemingly impossible tasks. By now I hope you know that you're under my aegis. Trust that I will always look out for you as best I can. Are you ready?"

"Yes," Lucio answered.

Leonardo handed Lucio a silver parchment tied with gold string. I suddenly remembered from my last assignment, so long ago, that these were how the orders were handed out. Lucio opened the scroll and read it to us.

Five simple words: Julian Miller, 45, Sunrise, Florida.

"You've got to be kidding me," Lucio said. "That's pretty close to where I lived in my last life."

"Now close your eyes," Leonardo said, and with that I, Lucio, and Serene fell into a sort of sleep.

CHAPTER 35

When I awoke, I felt like I was dreaming. Everything seemed very unreal. Unlike my one and only other assignment, I didn't wake up in water, but instead standing on the side of a road.

Earth was not as bright as I had remembered. The green of the grass and bushes we stood near seemed flat next to the bright emerald of the Realm. We were on the edge of what seemed to be a busy road, with fast and noisy metal contraptions roaring past us. The noise startled me, and I hopped backwards, realizing just at that moment that these must be automobiles. I had seen pictures in the library and had heard other angels' stories about them. A car had caused Serene's death, and I couldn't understand why she wasn't jumping back from the road too.

Instead, she and Lucio burst out laughing.

"Boy, you've got to put on some clothes there," Serene said. "I mean, we know you, but not *that* well yet."

I looked down and realized, to my horror, that I was stark naked again, like I had been on my first assignment. I quickly covered my crotch with my hands.

"Gross," Lucio said. "Come on, man. Did you forget to concentrate on clothing? It's the first thing you have to do when you get back to Earth. I just figured you'd remember that from your first assignment."

Quickly, I began meditating, until once again I was wearing my nineteenth-century garb. If people could see me, they would think I was in costume. Serene and Lucio's clothes were more appropriate to the twenty-first century.

"Much better," Lucio said. Suddenly a roar came from the skies, and I jumped, while Serene laughed again. There, soaring across the sky, was a monstrous bird of flight that roared like a dragon. It was an airplane, another invention I had never experienced in person.

"It's just an airplane, silly," Serene said. "Surely you read up and saw pictures of them during your studies."

"Yes. But they're so loud."

We stood there a minute, peering across the road at a huge enclosed structure that was surrounded by cars.

"Where are we?" I asked.

"I think I've been here," Lucio said.

"Really?" Serene asked.

"Well, that over there," he said, referring to the gargantuan group of interconnected buildings that lay across the road from us, "that is Sawgrass Mills Mall, and in my last life, I lived south of here in Miami-Dade County."

"Are you okay with that?" I asked, worried that maybe like me, Lucio would be distracted by unfinished business in his old home."

"It is what it is. Obviously South Florida is where Julian Miller lives, and you know that if we were put in this specific spot, there must be a tie-in to our assignment here. That's what we need to find out."

"Ooh, a mall. One of my favorite old hangouts," Serene said.

"It's not very glorious, is it," complained Lucio.

"To me it is," Serene said, laughing again. "I used to love hanging out at malls with my friends when I was alive. And it looks like that's where we need to go. Why else would they plop us down right across from it?"

"What's a mall?" I asked.

"Boy, this is going to be one long assignment if we have to explain everything to you," sighed Serene.

"I guess you didn't read up on malls during your time in the library," Lucio said. "Well, during your time there were stores . . . uh, shops, where things were sold, right?" he asked.

"Of course," I answered.

"A mall is just a place where a lot of stores are grouped together under one big roof."

"A gigantic one, if you ask me. Everything here seems oversized."

"Get used to it," Serene said. "You should see some of the people."

"Come on, let's go," Lucio said, drifting across the road. We followed, and minutes later we stood in the most crowded and hugest building I had ever been in. I froze in shock. Serene was right about the size of the people. While there were people of all sizes in the Realm, here they all just seemed taller and broader, and most of them were dressed totally inappropriately to my eyes. Some of the women, many quite young, showed their stomachs and wore shirts that barely covered partially exposed bosoms.

I couldn't help but stare. I had died inexperienced in the ways of the flesh, and I was now seeing more of girls' bodies in person than I had in the entire time I had lived. Some boys wore what seemed to be oversized and droopy pants and shirts; others wore very tight-fitting pants. Their personal undergarments were sometimes on display. Then there were the tattoos. Both sexes displayed tattoos, some quite large and tacky. The tattoos reminded me of some of the sailors aboard the whaler I had worked on so long, long ago.

My thoughts were interrupted by the laughter of Lucio and Serene.

"Are you going to be okay?" Lucio asked. "You seem freaked out."

"What do you mean?" I asked.

"Overwhelmed. You seem overwhelmed."

"Oh. Everything is . . . so noisy and inappropriate. Even though some of the dress in the Realm seemed odd to me, it wasn't as bad as this."

Serene smiled. "Believe it or not, a lot of people who live in these times feel like you do. But you'll get used to it," she said. "Well, Lucio, what now?"

"I suppose we'll have to explore this mall. Let's just walk around."

"Sounds good to me," said Serene. "But you know what I don't get? Although I've been an angel for two years now, I still can't accept why they have to be so vague all the time. Like, why can't they just tell us where to find this Julian guy?"

"Serene, remember what Leonardo told us," Lucio said. "We're appointed angels, not created ones, so we have to prove ourselves, and figuring this out is one of the ways we do that."

"Yeah, whatever, but if this is such an important assignment, you'd think they'd make an exception."

"They put us right here, didn't they? It'll be obvious. You'll see."

Thus we began to drift around the massive mall called Sawgrass Mills. We walked through a series of tall, tunnel-like corridors that were numbered and marked with high signs that read Entering Four, Entering One. Although structurally the building was unlike anything I had ever been in, it was the products for sale that captured my interest and awe. Seeing these items in person, and not just reading about or seeing pictures of them, made me believe that magic finally existed on Earth.

Among the proofs of this were the boxes and tiny contraptions from which pictures and voices emerged. I had read up on and seen these inventions during my studies in the Realm, but seeing them in use here on Earth was different. There were even these clear crystal blocks that had images of people or places floating in them. It was amazing.

I had so many questions, but I kept them to myself. I didn't want to become a burden to the team and bother them with too many queries, so I just followed the others as we drifted from one end of the enormous mall to the other, with Serene running into some of the stores to examine the clothing.

Eventually Lucio found what we were looking for. It was, as he had predicted, obvious. Of all the stores selling clothes, shoes, and beds, and so many items that I didn't understand, there was only one that might be considered angelic. While the entrance to the Psychic Fair Emporium sported a large green dragon and a wand-extending wizard, much of the store was dedicated to angels—angel statues, angel coins, angel art, and, most importantly, angel stones.

So we began our quest by just sitting inside the store and observing who went in and out.

It was sort of ironic, watching customers stroll past us, looking intently through angel paraphernalia and not realizing that nearby were three real angels. I never got a sense that any of the customers noticed us until the next day, after we had spent a long night in the shop. Lucio and Serene slept a while, even though we didn't need to, but I felt so energetic, with all the excitement from being on Earth again, that I just stayed awake. That morning, after the staff opened the store, I couldn't contain myself, and I yelled out to a family who had just walked in.

"We're right here," I said, laughing.

Then, surprisingly, a toddler in a stroller, who couldn't have been more than three, looked straight at us. "Mama," he said, tugging at his mother's trousers and pointing at us with his other hand. "Real angels."

She looked where he pointed, but her blank expression proved she had neither heard nor seen me. "Now, now, Ricky," she said, pulling him towards another section of the store. "Come help me pick out a nice statue for Nana."

"He heard you," said Lucio when they had walked away. "You need to be aware of when you speak. You know that your voice has power."

"I like it," Serene said. "Use it for fun. Freak someone out."

"Serene! We're not here to play games," Lucio admonished.

"It'd be better than all this waiting around doing nothing," she complained.

So the hours came and went and came and went, and still we had no sense of what we were supposed to do.

We did have time to learn all about the store and its employees. There were a total of five workers, plus three psychics who gave readings to customers. The three daytime workers were Ralph, Maria, and C.J.

C.J. was the oldest, a sprightly, petite woman with a radiant smile and uplifting energy that rubbed off on those around her. She was in charge of her young co-workers, who spent their days listening to energetic music and helping customers.

The evening staff was the total opposite of the bubbly day staff. No music filled the store at night, and the two workers, Paul and Asia, seemed very serious. Paul was a rather introverted man who had odd habits, like breaking into what seemed to be Native American chants at random, sometimes awkward times, leaving Asia and the customers rather perplexed. Asia was serious but kind and always had time to help her co-workers or customers.

Then there were the psychics: Will, a rotund man who specialized in tarot readings; Jacqueline, a pretty redhead who read palms; and Ned, who claimed he could read people's auras but who somehow failed to notice us.

As the time passed, Serene finally explained to me many of the items I had seen for sale in the mall, like iPhones and plasma television sets and "magical" cubes that were actually just something called 3-D laser crystals. In 150 years, the Earth had changed quite a bit, and I wondered what it would be like to be reborn into this time period.

Appointed angels in our particular realm were sometimes offered rebirth after completing a certain number of assignments. I wasn't sure if I would take the chance of being reborn into this time period. It seemed too noisy and too crass. But then my thoughts turned to Henry again. Had he been reborn? If so, how would I meet up with him and recognize him? I had no idea where he was in this grand universe or if we would ever reunite. I suddenly felt sad, but I had to snap myself out of it. *Keep focused*, I urged myself. I could not allow myself to think of Henry now.

"Do you think you'd ever want to be reborn?" I asked, trying to distract myself. "Have either of you had the option?"

"Yes," Lucio replied. "Two times. The Council gave me two chances to be reborn again, and I turned them down each time."

"You turned the chance down, but why?" Serene asked. "I'd jump at the chance."

"Because my last life wasn't my only life, and I'm tired of dying and, strangely enough, tired of living. Even the chance of a long, easy life doesn't entice me; at least not yet. So here I am."

"So you know what your other lives have been like?" I asked in awe.

"Yes," he answered. "And they have been troubled. You see, I was not a good person during my first life."

"You remember it?"

"Not really. I found out about it, and it's not something I'm proud of."

"You've never told me about this. What happened?" Serene asked. Lucio looked away, as if debating whether to tell us or not, but then decided he would.

"I was part of a band of marauders that invaded a village, and I set fire to what turned out to be the village's nursery. I caused the death of many innocent babies—twelve souls to be exact. Twelve who should have lived. And so my other lives have been mostly a penance for that act."

"What were your lives like?" Serene asked.

"I've been a soldier, a baker, a candlestick maker . . . Just kidding," he said, when he noticed our expressions. "Maybe some other time I'll give you all the details, but let's just say that I've died young quite a few times, and I've experienced a few world wars."

"Interesting. So you were part of those great wars," I said.

After all my studying, I had noticed that history seemed to repeat itself in a sense, but always on a larger scale. I had been Earthbound during those great conflicts, but I hadn't been aware of anything other than the darkness. My mind brimmed with questions. How had Lucio found out about his past lives? What about the people he'd loved during those lives? Had he seen them since? But just as I got ready to ask him, a woman walked through the door.

CHAPTER 36

"My God, is that you? Julianne Miller!" C.J. yelled out at the rather striking young woman who had entered the store. "It's been so long, my dear."

The human we'd been sent to find was not at all what we expected. Miller was not a Julian, but a Julianne—a woman. And what a woman she was. When she walked in, it was like a ray of sunshine caught the attention of everyone in the store. She had long, silky, radiantly blond hair and an almost magical face, like that of some fairy princess. She was delicate, almost birdlike; she reminded me of a Siren, one of the temptresses of ancient Greek sailors.

"Wow. Even angels' orders can have typos," laughed Serene.

"You're right about that," Lucio answered, staring intently at Julianne.

"Typos?" I asked.

They ignored me. I suppose the name and Gabriel's description of what Miller was doing had drawn in my mind a picture of a rather foreboding man. Instead, Julianne was exquisite. Lucio could not stop staring at her.

Julianne walked up to C.J. and just looked at her, and C.J. stared back, not saying anything more at first. Then, "My God," C.J. said again. "Tell me your secret, your doctor's name. You look twenty years younger."

"Just some things I've been doing," muttered Julianne.

"Do you want me to start up your appointments with Will again? He tells me he's missed you."

"Not yet," Julianne said. "Things are going better for me now; I don't need to see him."

"You do look so good, my dear, and I'm so happy to see you like this after everything you've gone through. We were worried when you stopped showing up for your weekly sessions, but then Will said he called you and you were just taking a break. I'm glad to see you've made so much progress in your recovery."

"C.J., have you gotten any more angel stones like the two you sold me?"

"No. Unfortunately, that supplier has never come back again."

"You must contact him," Julianne demanded.

"It's been months. I don't know what I might have done with his business card."

"You'll find it," Julianne said. "And you'll call that supplier by this weekend and let me know by early next week."

As I watched her, a dark glint seemed to appear in the blue of her eyes.

"Yes, I will," C.J. responded, as if in a trance. With that, Julianne strolled out of the shop, with Lucio still staring at her.

"That was weird," said Serene to Lucio. "What do you think?"

But Lucio didn't answer; he just stared.

"I can't believe that was Julianne," said Ralph, rushing up to C.J. "How young she looks! I thought Harry's death had devastated her."

"Me too. I don't know how, but she's changed so drastically." C.J. answered. "She's not the woman we used to know."

Lucio, Serene, and I looked at each other. "The stones. She has two of them. What's your guess?" Serene asked.

"Which stones were missing?" asked Lucio.

"Health," I said. "Maybe that's one of the ones she has. Those people just mentioned how much healthier she looks. The other stolen stones were Youth, Bravery, and Longevity, and one more that I can't remember."

"Persuasion," added Serene. "She *is* persuasive."

"Well, maybe she has all of them," said Lucio. "They pretty much fit."

"Yes, but Gabriel told us she only had two."

"Well, I would say Youth—she's obviously much older than she looks, and C.J. said she had changed. And maybe it is Persuasion. She sure got the old lady to agree to track down some guy for her," Lucio said.

"Do you think it was Jared who came in and sold those stones to the store?" I asked.

"I don't know, and Gabriel didn't tell us, but I think this means we need to follow two courses of action now," Lucio said. "This is what we'll do. Serene, you'll stay here at the store to see if C.J. contacts this source of the stones, and Nic and I will follow Julianne."

"What? I have to stay here alone?" Serene complained.

"Yes. I think it's best if one of us stays to keep an eye on what happens concerning the stones." Serene, looking displeased, motioned for Lucio to come nearer to her. It was obvious she didn't want me to hear what she whispered to him, so, feeling like an intruder, I walked away.

I still heard some of their discussion. "Can't he . . . here? You've known . . . longer."

"Look, Serene, he needs to be with me," Lucio answered loudly, obviously irritated. "As team leader, I make the decisions. Stay here until we return."

So we left a displeased Serene at the store, and Lucio and I left the Psychic Emporium to follow Julianne Miller, who had already reached the end of a long corridor of stores.

"I could have stayed," I said to Lucio, hoping to make the situation less awkward.

"I didn't want her to come," Lucio snapped back.

I decided then to just follow his orders. We hoped of course that Julianne would lead us straight to her home, so that we could at least see where the angels were, but that was not to be.

CHAPTER 37

Lucio and I sat in the back of Julianne's car—a large red vehicle. She had swung open a large door in the back to stow a bag she was carrying, and Lucio and I crawled quickly past her into the rear space. I was silent, in fear that Julianne would hear me, but it was funny that she didn't know she had two angels for passengers, and I found myself laughing inwardly at the thought. I knew Lucio thought it amusing too, for soon enough he laughed aloud. Julianne could not hear him, and so we continued on a ride I found both exhilarating and nerve-racking.

I had obviously never been in such a contraption, and now I found myself in this metal casement speeding down a road onto what looked like a concrete mountain filled with other speeding vehicles. I couldn't believe how fast we traveled, couldn't believe that a single person was capable of maneuvering such a thing. When, during the voyage, Julianne began punching some buttons on a music-emitting box at the front of her car, I thought that surely we would fly off the road. Not that it would have hurt Lucio or me, but it's not easy to lose all the reactions you acquire during life. However, Julianne took every curve with ease. By the time we got off the mountain and back onto the lower roads, I noticed Lucio was staring at me.

We ended up on a brightly lit road, bordered by what seemed to be a mile-long jumble of taverns and shops that fronted a large beach area. Julianne turned into a parking lot near one of the outdoor taverns—a place called Nick's; funny how it was named like me—a squat building with a performance stage, tables, and a large open patio area that faced the ocean. We stepped out of the car and watched Julianne head towards the front entrance.

"Did you like the ride?" Lucio asked. "What do you think of cars?"

"It was different," I answered. "The speed is amazing, almost like the thrill I experienced when the *Mary Selina* was clipping along. So, what now? Do we follow her and just keep watching?"

"Yes and no," Lucio said.

"Huh?"

"Well for you, yes. But for me, well, Julianne is going to get to know me tonight. And you're going to learn about my skills, which I've never told you about."

"What do you mean?"

"She's going to see me as if I was alive," Lucio said. He walked off, and I followed him into the tavern, amazed that Lucio was at a level where he could appear to living people as if he were one of them.

Nick's was packed with an assortment of people. There were groups of men drinking liquor and eyeing the girls in short skirts and low-cut blouses, as well as middle-aged couples, some who looked like they'd lost their passion and barely looked at each other anymore. There were rowdy drunks and couples who kissed openly in public. So this was life now— different, yet still, like in my time, a mosaic of lovers, friends, and family. I felt that yearning again to see Henry, and suddenly

I thought also of my mother and father. I wondered if I would ever stop missing them.

I worked my way through the crowd until I stood next to Julianne, who of course could not see me at all. She ordered two large red drinks, which she drank while assorted guys nearby tried to converse with her. She didn't seem interested in any of them, and her short, rather unfriendly responses put them off. Lucio had strolled away, saying that when he returned he would be visible to all, and I wondered how he expected to have any better luck talking to Julianne, who obviously wanted to be left alone.

Then I noticed that Julianne's attention had been captured by someone. Her eyes seemed brighter as she stared through the crowd in front of her. I peered over to see who it was and realized it was one of the workers, carrying a tray of drinks and busily meeting the demands of his clientele. When his work slowed, Julianne called him over. "Hey, Carl, how's it going tonight?" she asked.

"Busy as always, Julianne. What do you want?"

"Well, these two drinks will do just fine for now. But I wondered if you'd seen Blind Passion tonight."

"Not yet. But they should be here by now. As far as I know, they're scheduled to play Friday nights through the month."

"Well, look, make sure you call me next time they show up," she said, reaching into her purse and pulling out a small white card, along with a twenty-dollar bill.

"What do you want with the band, Juli? You never have told me. You've had a few chances to talk to them already, and instead you just sit here."

"I just like their sound. That's all."

"Okay. I'll call you," Carl said, smiling down at the bill in his hand. "But you might as well stick around a little longer; they might still show up."

"Okay," Julianne said, settling down on her bar stool again.

"Do you want this back?" he asked, handing back the bill.

"Keep it, just in case, for next time," she said.

As the minutes passed, the tavern seemed to get more crowded and noisy, but then in a split second there was a change in the air. Something or someone of importance had arrived. Julianne noticed it too, looking up from her handbag, which she had been digging through. By the time I looked up, I knew it was Lucio who was causing all the commotion.

Lucio's energy emitted such a strong presence that he'd become a cynosure, with many in the packed bar staring at him as he walked by—dressed quite twenty-first-century stylish in rather tight blue jeans and a button-down pink shirt! He was a handsome young man, but in this angel-turned-human state, his handsomeness had a luminous quality about it, sort of like the subjects in John William Waterhouse paintings I had seen in a book in the Realm's library. Julianne was not immune. Neither was I. Even as I became upset with myself for feeling attracted to him, I followed him as he walked by, not stopping.

"Hey, hey, I thought you were going to talk to her," I whispered, hoping no one would hear me.

"I know. I know. I'm just kind of anxious," he said, looking around to see if anyone was watching him talk to what seemed empty air. "It's been a while since I've been in this type of situation, and, well, her beauty is kind of off-putting. She makes me nervous."

"Well you have to, Lucio. Serene and I can't do this."

"You're right. Okay, I'll do it," he said, more to himself than to me. He turned around and marched right up to her.

"Do you mind if I squeeze in here," he said, obviously uncomfortable.

"I guess," she said. His appeal was obviously irresistible, because Julianne, who had sent every other possible suitor off, seemed enchanted, and she suddenly smiled.

He introduced himself, and they began to talk. As Julianne opened up to Lucio about herself, she seemed to capture him with her looks and soothing, singsong voice; again she reminded me of a Siren casting a spell on her young suitor.

They talked for over an hour. We learned that Julianne worked with computers, which I still didn't quite understand. She was divorced and had a son named Harry. Though she seemed reluctant to give many details about what had happened, we found out that he had passed away the year before.

Julianne looked no older than twenty-five, yet our angel order said she was forty-five. I realized then that it had to be the power of the angel stone. Her son had probably been a lot older than she was letting on to Lucio.

Lucio too started talking, about what I figured had been his real life on Earth. He told her he worked as an automobile mechanic, but that his real love was art, and he specialized in fantasy art. Julianne seemed quite impressed with that. She was obviously attracted to Lucio, judging by the way she leaned in as she talked to him.

As the evening progressed, and Lucio and Julianne continued drinking, things became even stranger, at least to my angel eyes. At one point she stared into Lucio's eyes, and I could tell that he too was feeling attracted to her, and then she moved closer to him and kissed him. I knew that we, being of the lowest realm of angels, could have physical relationships with others in the Realm, but I had never imagined we could be physical with a living human. But then I remembered that not all of us could. I couldn't. It was only angels who could be seen and touched, like Lucio, who could do that.

I wondered what Leonardo would think about this. I also wondered how the living felt when they kissed us. At first Lucio seemed uncomfortable; he broke off the kiss and glanced at me, but then she moved in closer, and it was like he couldn't resist. They both gave in to the enjoyment of the kiss, a long, protracted event that, after a while, made me feel like a voyeur. I wished I had stayed with Serene at the shop.

Then suddenly a loud noise from the stage interrupted Lucio and Julianne's moment. When I looked, some young men were fixing some contraptions onto the stage. One was a long silver pole with a black cover on top of it, and there were big black boxes, to which they were attaching a series of wires. They had instruments that looked to be guitars, but shinier than any I had ever seen, and then they plugged some of the wires into them.

I glanced over at Lucio, and he motioned for me to look at Julianne. Everything about her had changed. She stared at the stage with a look that could only be described as venomous. There were four young men on stage, but her eyes were focused on the one at the front, who was working with the wires. Later I found out he was the singer. He was tall, dark, and handsome in a most princely way. He looked to be about eighteen, with long jet-black hair and deep blue eyes. For a moment he locked eyes with Julianne, and his quizzical expression suddenly reminded me of Henry.

"Are you okay?" Lucio asked Julianne.

"Yes, I'm fine."

"You're staring at the band. Do you know them?"

"No," she snapped. Then, composing herself, she said, "I just remembered something. But look, here's my card. I really would love to see you again, Lucio. Call me. We'll meet up here again."

"Wait, you don't want to stay for the show?"

"Not tonight. But you enjoy it. They're quite good, although they used to be better."

With that, she got up and walked away, just as the band began to play some rather harsh-sounding music on their instruments. At first I found the music irritating, at times almost ear-shattering, but after a while, I began to enjoy its energy and pulsing beat, and I could understand why some people had gotten up to dance. Even if they were doing so in a way that was very strange to my eyes.

"Well, that was weird," Lucio said loudly.

It would be easier for us to speak now because of the noise and everyone's focus on the stage. People wouldn't think he was some crazy person speaking to himself.

"What?"

"You know. How she just left. We know she was waiting for them. And what was that crack about them being 'better' before?"

"Why would she leave?" I asked.

"I don't know. Maybe my presence threw off her plans. Look, I'm going to make myself invisible again and follow her. You stay here, stick with the band, find out what you can, and I'll meet you back here. And I'll find a way to get us back to Serene and the shop."

So my orders were set, and I waited and waited until the band finished playing, which was hours later. Blind Passion took their time packing up their instruments and supplies while sharing smiles and conversation with assorted young women. Eventually, though, all but one of the musicians left the bar together and ended up at another nearby tavern, sitting at an enclosed table, eating breakfast, and talking about their evening.

Along with the singer, whose name turned out to be David, Blind Passion consisted of a burly blond boy named Mack, a reed-thin guy named Tim, who had a face filled with scars, and a fourth musician, Diego, who had, as the others said, "gotten lucky" with some girl and wasn't around. For much of the meal, the conversation focused on their performance, but then they started talking about Julianne.

"Did you see that lady was back again?" Tim asked. "Every time we perform at Nick's, she's there, and she always looks pissed."

"Yeah, I saw her glaring at me," David said. "It creeps me out. It's like she's stalking us."

"Maybe she has a secret crush on you," Mack joked. "She's pretty hot."

"You're kidding, right?" said David irritably. "Those are not glances of love."

"Who is she?" Mack asked.

"I'm not sure," David said, "but she reminds me of Harry's mom. Except much younger, so it can't be her."

"I guess. The only time I saw Harry's mom was at the viewing," Tim commented.

"That was a mistake, going to that," Mack said.

David nodded. "Damn right. She tossed us out of there. But I don't know, maybe she was right. We probably shouldn't have gone."

"Come on, David," Mack said. "How long are you going to blame yourself for what Harry did? It just didn't work out, that's all. He wasn't the first guy to ever get fired from a band. The guy was whacked."

"Yes, but I should have seen it coming. He'd been acting so strange, and I made fun of him, egged him on. My kicking him out of the band just finally took him over the edge."

"His suicide is not your fault. You didn't know he would do something so drastic. You did what you had to do," Mack said.

"I guess," said David, unconvincingly.

I realized I had a vital piece of information to share with Lucio and Serene. This Harry they were talking about, who had killed himself after being fired from the band, must be Julianne's dead son. I left the band and walked back to Nick's, which was only a few blocks away, but when I got there, it was close to dawn and the place was closed, so I waited outside for Lucio.

Fortunately, it wasn't long before Lucio showed up again, getting out of a yellow car that had pulled up to the front. The car had the word *TAXI* written on it next to a series of numbers. Lucio stepped out of the car and then handed the driver what looked to be currency. Then the car just waited there, and Lucio waved me to follow him out of view of the driver. I suppose Lucio could read the quizzical expression on my face because he immediately explained.

"That's a taxi, a vehicle that will get us back to the mall. Before I took my live form tonight, I contacted Leonardo and told him I would need money to get by. He of course provided me with an adequate amount. Once we get back to the mall, I'll go invisible again. So for now just follow me."

"I have something important to tell you," I stated.

"Tell me when we get back."

Because the mall was closed, the taxi dropped us off down the street, and Lucio once again paid the driver. Then, as we walked towards the massive structure, I realized that something was happening to Lucio. His luminous quality was fading, and he looked, well, regular to me again.

"I'm invisible again," he finally said. The mall was locked, and there was no way for us to enter, so we were forced to spend the rest of the night outside, where we fell asleep under some palm trees next to a front entrance.

CHAPTER 38

Dawn came, and the doors of the mall were finally unlocked. We followed a man in who was dressed in a gray uniform and finally made our way back to the angel shop, where we reunited with Serene.

"Where the hell were you?" she snapped. "I got worried when you didn't return."

"We got back late and got locked out," Lucio said. We told her everything that had happened at the tavern, and then we took turns sharing what we each individually had learned. I explained how Julianne's son, Harry, had played for the band at one point but had committed suicide when they asked him to leave.

"That's pretty traumatic," said Serene. "Perhaps that situation is somehow tied to the stones."

"I agree," said Lucio, whose quest had also been fruitful. Following Julianne in an invisible state, he had found out that for some reason, Julianne wasn't staying at her house but was living temporarily with a friend.

"At first I thought I was at her house, but then her roommate kept asking her how much longer she was going to be there. That the original three-month agreement they'd had had turned to five. Julianne begged her friend to give her another couple of weeks. Said the work on her home would definitely be completed by then, something about some inter-wall plumbing work being done. I'm not sure if I believe her. There was something about what she was saying that just didn't ring true to me."

"You think she plans to do something within the next few weeks, and it has to do with the angels," Serene said.

"I have no idea, but she was asking C.J. for more power stones. What type of stones were they again?"

"If I remember, Gabriel said they were Youth, Persuasion, Longevity, Health, and Bravery," I answered.

"And she has two," said Lucio. "Which two make the most sense?"

"Well, she has youth and she is persuasive. She doesn't seem sick or poor. Maybe she wants something that would help her with whatever she wants to do to David. She's obviously tracking him."

"I think you're right," said Lucio. "There was hatred in her eyes when she stared at David. He may be in danger. You two stay here tomorrow and see if C.J. goes through with her promise to call the stone supplier. I'm going to call Julianne tomorrow and try to make a date. I need to get her to take me to her real home."

"A date?" Serene said in an accusatory tone. It was more than a question.

"He let her see him, and she ended up fancying him, I think," I said, realizing right away that I should have remained silent.

"What?" snapped Serene.

"Look, Serene, I have to get close to her to be able to influence her to give me the stones. Remember, Gabriel said she must turn over the stones by herself."

"So you got close? What, physically?" She glared at Lucio.

"I have to have some sort of relationship with her to make this work," he said.

"Whatever," said Serene, and walked off.

I realized then that Serene might care for Lucio more than he cared for her. How was that going to impact our work?

"You shouldn't have opened your mouth like that," Lucio snapped. "Now she's upset."

"Don't blame me," I said. "I don't know what your relationship is with Serene, but I don't think you're acting like a gentleman. If you and Serene are a couple of sorts, I foresee some complications."

"Serene and I are not a couple. She's a wonderful person, and of course she's pretty, and we kissed once, but I realized my feelings for her weren't like that. She's a close friend. Plus, Julianne means nothing. She's an attractive woman, and I have a job to do, and I will do what I have to do to make it succeed."

"A job? That's an interesting way to see it. A gentleman doesn't treat women like that. You can't just go around kissing someone if it doesn't mean anything."

Lucio smiled at me. "Is that what this is about?" he asked. "Look, Nic, things are different in the twenty-first century. Kissing and even having sex with someone isn't necessarily a big deal now. People have sex all the time with people they don't marry or even have a deep relationship with."

"Really?"

"Yes, really."

"Well, times have changed. Girls who did such things in our time were thought of as Jezebels. And a gentleman would never use a nice girl."

"Well, it's not that way anymore."

I was shocked. But then, what would I know? I had never found myself pining for any girl during my sixteen years of life; I had died innocent, mostly because I was . . . Still, I found

Lucio's behavior distasteful. "So what will you do, just take advantage of Julianne, as you have Serene?"

I regretted saying it the minute it left my mouth. Perhaps I was being too harsh.

"Don't be ridiculous," Lucio said angrily. "You, really, *you* of all people are going to judge me?"

His words stung, and so I remained silent. He was right. After all, I was the one who had fallen.

I walked away, to the back of the store, and remained there for the rest of the morning. I wanted to be by myself. But the situation was still awkward at the end of the day. Lucio and Serene were barely speaking, and I found I didn't want to say much to them either. Lucio coldly ordered Serene and me to continue to wait and see if C.J. contacted the stone dealer. We followed Lucio's orders and sat near C.J., watching her peruse a stack of cards that had people's names and phone numbers on them. Serene was in a bad mood.

"This is a total waste of time," she said, looking grim. "She's not going to call anyone. I hope Lucio isn't making us do this just so he can spend time alone with Julianne."

"He's just working on the assignment," I said, trying to comfort her.

"I hope he's not falling for her. I know what a mistake that would be. I almost fell in love with my first assignment, and since then I've heard several stories about angels who turned to the darkness because they fell in love and refused to return to the Realm. It's useless though. Even if we were like Lucio, who can be seen on Earth, once an assignment ends, our visibility ends about a month later. We would basically become spirits haunting the people we love."

"Like me and Henry," I whispered.

"What did you say?" Serene asked.

"Nothing."

"Gosh, I can't believe this would happen," she continued.

"Serene, this is just an assignment for him."

"I thought he liked me," she said quietly.

"He does care for you; you're his friend," I said, realizing I was only making her feel worse. "I'm sorry."

I was about to continue when C.J. suddenly yelled out. "Ralph, I found the supplier of those stones Julianne was interested in. I think I'll call him."

We looked over at the card in her hand. It read: José Basca, Angel Stone Dealer Extraordinaire.

"Do you think José works with Jared?" I asked Serene.

"Perhaps. This could get interesting."

So we listened in as C.J. made her appointment. "No, I can't wait until Thursday the fourteenth," she said over the phone. "If you want to make a deal with us, you need to come by this weekend. One of our clients is interested. . . . Which one? Her name is Julianne. . . . Okay, that sounds good. I'll see you then."

"What happened?" Ralph asked, walking over.

"He's coming in tomorrow morning at ten."

Serene and I just stared at each other.

CHAPTER 39

The next morning, a Sunday, José Basca walked into the shop carrying a wide black case. I, unfortunately, was left alone to deal with this important situation. Lucio had not yet returned from his meeting with Julianne on Saturday night, and Serene, who had become increasingly upset as the hours passed, stormed out of the shop at midnight. I knew she was thinking what I was—that Lucio had somehow become more seriously and physically involved with Julianne.

I had to decide what to do, and it scared me. I worried that I might make a mistake, and I worried about this whole assignment and why the masters had put our team together in the first place. There was me, the fallen one, and now Lucio and Serene had disappeared, and the whole situation seemed so scattered. My fears would have to wait, though, because Basca was now in front of me.

Basca was a bear-shaped man with thick, black-framed glasses that adorned a rather cute, whimsical face. He carried an air of mischievousness in his eyes and smiling mouth. "Hello, my dear C.J.," he said, kissing her on both cheeks. "It's been a while my dear. You know how time flies."

"Yes, I do. So what do you have for me?"

"I think you'll be pleasantly surprised," he said. "Last time I only had five of these particular stones, but now . . ."

He opened the case, and my mouth dropped open. Five rows of boxes folded out, each successive row folding past another. Each row held four individual boxes, and each box was marked with its own special power. There was Beauty and Intelligence, Inquiry and Peace, Athleticism and so on.

Somehow Basca was holding twenty power stones? How could this be? Was Jared still stealing stones? I wondered if anyone in the Realm knew of this. They must, surely. But if so, why hadn't we been told?

"Wow, new ones," C.J. said. "My client is definitely interested."

"Well, the price has risen on these types of stones since she last purchased them. Make sure you tell her that. My supplier doesn't know how many more he'll be able to give me. So this set may be the last."

C.J. reached for a box marked Passion and opened it. She pulled out a clear stone about the size of a peach pit. For all its power, the stone seemed rather ordinary, or so I thought at first, but as C.J. held the clear stone in the palm of her hand, a flicker of red arose from its center, like the flame of a candle. It diminished, then rose again. "Ooh," said C.J. "I just felt a rush of energy. I might want to buy one of these."

Basca quickly snatched the stone out of her hand.

"Not now. Jared makes the final decisions on sales. I'd have to ask him. We'll be back Tuesday morning at nine o'clock to complete the transaction in person with Julianne."

"And you, of course, will give the store its cut for the sale," said C.J.

"Yes. Thirty percent, as before, and with the price hike, you'll make a hefty profit."

"I still don't know why you can't just sell us the lot for a fair wholesale price," C.J. said. "I'm sure we could sell them off quickly."

"It will be done this way," Basca said. "My supplier wants control in the process. He'll come in again to talk to her, like he did last time. He only allows sales to those he feels worthy. If you want a stone, C.J, he'll have to interview you."

"It's the oddest thing I ever heard of," C.J said. "It was weird then, and it's weird now. He's a strange bird, he is."

"You might say that."

"How did you come to work with him?"

"I need to go now," Basca said, obviously not wanting to answer. "We'll be here Tuesday."

I watched him leave, hoping that by Tuesday, Serene and Lucio would be back from wherever they were.

CHAPTER 40

My hopes were moot. On Monday, Lucio and Serene were still missing, and I was starting to panic. Where were they? This team was unraveling, and I was left alone to make decisions I didn't feel qualified to make. What was I supposed to do when Jared appeared? The only thing I knew was that I had to let the Realm know about Jared stealing more angel stones. I contemplated contacting Leonardo, then decided against it. I didn't want him knowing about the disarray of our team and feared that Gabriel would find out.

Instead I decided to contact Magellan. After all, we had been good friends since I had returned to the Realm. It was he who took me back to the Realm after Henry's home was torn down, and he who helped with my recovery, letting me live in his chalet. So I would contact him in the manner in which we angels could communicate while on Earth.

It took a while. I spent all morning thinking and reaching out mentally to Magellan in hopes he would come to me. By late afternoon, he did, appearing first as a white ball of energy that I thought only I could see—until I noticed a young girl staring at it. Then the light transformed into the Magellan I knew. I realized the girl could not see Magellan in this form because she walked away, shaking her head perplexedly.

"Hello, my young friend," he greeted me warmly. "What has occurred that you so strongly summoned me here today? I was busy planting some roses. I think I need more color in the front of my home."

"I'm sorry, Magellan. But everything is a mess. I don't know where the others are, and I have some important news for the Realm."

"Why didn't you just contact Leonardo? He is your master."

"Yes, but I didn't want to let him know about the problems we're having. I can't afford for anyone in the Realm to think I'm failing here."

"You worry too much about what others think, Nicolas. I have faith in you, as you well should. You will succeed."

"It's doubtful. Serene and Lucio have disappeared."

"That is not acceptable," Magellan said. "You are a team and should know what one and the other are doing. Who is in charge?"

"Lucio."

"What did he say when he left?" Magellan asked.

"He told us to stay here."

"Then you should have both listened. One has to listen to the leader. That's what caused me so many problems in my lifetime. Now, what happened with Serene?"

"She was upset with Lucio and walked away. She hasn't come back."

"I see you're in a quandary."

"And that's not the worst of it. Can you get a message to Gabriel for me?"

"Nicolas, you should know I'm not allowed at that level yet and have no contact with those at that level. This *is* going to have to go through Leonardo."

"Please, you have to help me. Just tell him I missed you and wanted to see you again, and that I have learned that Jared has somehow managed to steal more of the power stones. He'll know what I'm talking about."

"Oh, Nicolas, you are worrying for no reason. We already know of that. More angels have been weakened by this action, and several of them have been trapped."

"Why didn't you tell us this was happening?"

"Nicolas, your assignment has nothing to do with these other stones and angels. You, Lucio, and Serene are to concentrate on the Miller situation and rescue the two angels who are trapped. Stay focused on that."

"I'm trying," I said. "But I'm not sure I know what to do."

Magellan gently squeezed my shoulder and smiled at me. "I have faith," he said.

I smiled at his kindness but still did not feel confident. I realized I had no choice. If the others didn't return, I would be forced to decide what course of action to take on my own.

"Thank you," I said.

"Now," Magellan said, "I will return to the Realm, but you and your team members must reunite and successfully complete the assignment."

With those words, Magellan slowly faded and disappeared. I realized I would probably have to face Jared alone. I did not sleep that night, but instead sat up, near a shelf filled with small fairy figurines.

My thoughts were with Henry. I had a picture of him in my mind. We were sitting in the hidden room at his home, playing cards and laughing at how we'd scared some of the Rodericks' neighbors when we played that silly haunting joke. In my mind, I saw him as young, alive, fun, and kind, like Henry always was when we were together, sharing our grand friendship. Not like when I'd said my last words to him, when I had so cruelly tortured him. Not suffering, as I last saw him when he took his own life.

"I wish you were here with me," I whispered to no one. So much of my life had been with Henry, and I wished that my afterlife could be too. "Where are you?" I asked, knowing it was a useless question.

Even though I had been warned not to dwell on Henry, there was a sort of strength my thoughts now gave me. Feelings washed over me like waves on a shoreline. "Everything has happened for a reason, Nic," Henry once said. In my head, I heard those words now, almost as clearly as then. When I had complained about the mistake I'd made by agreeing to join him on the *Mary Selina*, he'd said, "You'll see, we'll learn from this experience." But what had we learned? I had learned that he would betray me to save his own skin, and that I could turn into a monster of vengeance. It had all turned out so horrible. I wondered then if this assignment would turn out just as bad.

CHAPTER 41

The next day, Julianne appeared, looking fresh and striking in a long green peasant-style gown. She carried her false youth well, and I could understand why Lucio was enchanted with her blond brightness. I wondered where Lucio was, however. If he had been with her these past days, why he wasn't with her now?

For now, though, she was alone, getting stares from several men that were in the shop while C.J. tried to entertain her as they waited for José. Our wait lasted only a few minutes. Then a surge of dark energy came into the room, as if someone had sucked the air out while simultaneously turning the lights off. I looked towards the entrance, and it wasn't José Basca. There was a strange-looking man there. Impossibly tall and thin, he had orange-red hair and pale, sheer skin that contrasted shockingly with the blackest of eyes. He carried the same case José had days earlier. This was the source of the stones—this was Jared.

I got prickles all over my skin as I realized that somehow he was managing to retain a living form. How was this possible?

His assignment had ended months before. As he made his way towards C.J., I suddenly felt afraid.

"Hello, Ms. Jones," he said to C.J. "I know you expected my distributor, José, to be here as well, but he was unable to join us for our meeting today. Hello, Julianne. How nice to see you again. It has been months."

He stretched out a skeletal hand to her. She took his hand, looking slightly repulsed by the touch.

"What is it you need today, my dear?" he asked, bringing her hand to his lips and kissing it. Julianne looked like she was going to be ill.

"I'm interested in purchasing some additional stones," she said, pulling her hand away.

"But you—" He stopped abruptly, looked over at C.J., and then continued. "That's fine, but may I suggest we go elsewhere to discuss it? I'd like a drink. I'm suddenly very thirsty."

What was Jared up to? Why couldn't the sale take place in the store? I noticed I wasn't the only one questioning the request: C.J., her face uncertain, began protesting. "Don't go," she said. "You're welcome to use one of our psychic reading rooms. I'll bring you both soft drinks."

"Well, as long as it's only Juli and I, I suppose that will do. But I insist on privacy."

"Fine," C.J. said. It struck me then that he didn't want anyone watching what was about to happen. But no matter, for I was here, and for some reason he hadn't noticed me. Perhaps in his live form he could not sense my presence. Still, I would keep my distance. There was something creepy about Jared.

I followed them towards the back of the store, where the four small rooms were. He and Julianne walked into one, carrying their soft drinks, and he closed the door. I stayed outside and listened.

"You are doing well with my gifts," Jared said. "Look at you, you're marvelous. But it's good you contacted me, because I was getting ready to track you down. I have almost granted you immortality, and a beautiful one at that, but you know I'm still waiting for your final payment. You owe me. It's taken you too long, Julianne, to accomplish your assignment—the one we discussed when I sold you the first pair of stones. You know it's your desire, and it's the right thing to do. The boy deserves to die. He must pay for what he did to Harry."

Revenge! So Julianne was seeking some sort of revenge—like I had.

"I believe he must pay," Julianne said. "But why do you care? What is all this to you, other than money from the sale of your stones?"

"Your actions serve a purpose for me. And that is not your concern."

"Not my concern!" Julianne said, her voice rising. "It's all my concern. My house is a nightmare. The minute I brought these stones home, it became a haunted place. With the moaning, the cold, I can't even live there anymore. Why didn't you tell me?"

"Stop your whining, Julianne. These stones gave you what you wanted and what you require to accomplish your ultimate desire."

"You're right," Julianne whispered. "And that's why I'm here, Jared. I can't go through with it. Every time I see David, every time I see him performing, a storm of anger hits me, but then fear. I freeze up. I'm afraid to do anything but glare at him. I need your help."

"I do have one stone that might be an answer, my dear. Look. Look at Bravery."

I could hear the case being popped open. For a moment, there was silence. Then, "Okay, I'll buy it," Julianne said.

I so wanted to enter then, to see what was happening, that I pressed myself up against the door. All of a sudden, the door opened, and I realized what a mistake it had been to get so close. Jared stared at me with icy, dark eyes, like an endless abyss. I knew he could somehow see me, or sense my presence.

"Stay away."

I heard the silent warning in my head. As his eyes bore down on me, I was struck by an odd feeling, as if I was shrinking. Everything became foggy, and I felt an energy rushing towards me. Before I could react, the force hit me, and I felt as if I were suffocating. I couldn't move. I was trapped where I stood, and no matter how hard I tried to fight, Jared's dark energy was stronger than I was.

"Now go, Juli, do what you must," Jared said calmly, barely paying attention to the large wad of money he held in his hand. "If you don't, you will see me again."

As she and Jared walked towards the front of the store, he glanced back at me and gave me a cruel smile. Pure panic surged through my being. What if I was to be trapped here, like I was trapped before, for eons? I would rather my energy be forever destroyed; I could not bear being trapped again. Then I heard Jared's voice again. He was talking to C.J.

"Here's what I owe you from the sale," he said. "Oh, I think I left something back there. Would you mind if I head back to look for it?"

"Of course not," said C.J. "Be my guest."

I was suddenly afraid—he was coming back. He walked up to me. His skeletal appearance, ghastly pallor, and venomous stare made my skin prickle. He moved closer to my face, and I averted my eyes from the endless, dark pool of his. "Don't interfere with me," he hissed silently, his thoughts appearing in my head.

"Let me go," I whispered.

"It should be a familiar feeling, fallen one."

"How do you know me?" I asked. "I've never met you."

"Everyone in the Realm knows about you, Nicolas—the story of the young fallen Nicolas,—and half of them I'd bet expect you'll fall again."

How did he know that? I hated him then. I hated that he was probably telling me the truth.

"Now tell me, why are you here? For me? Or are you on another assignment? Either way, you're bound to fail, Nicolas. The masters know that, and when you fail, you'll be cast from the Realm, cast away forever this time. It's what they do. Didn't they warn you?"

Was he telling the truth?

"So tell me, Nicolas. What are you doing here?"

I was silent. I would tell him nothing.

"I'll find out, but I warn you, if you interfere with me again, you will pay, and this time for eternity. What does it feel like to be trapped again, huh? I know you spent many years in the dark, Nicolas. This must be like old times."

"Let me go," I said.

He laughed, like a crazy hyena, a silent laugh that I knew only I could hear and that sounded unnatural, like everything about him. Then he walked away. Time passed and I wept, for indeed I felt as if all was lost again. I thought too of the other angels he had trapped and their agony and how they must feel. For it had been months since they were ensnared, and they, like me, were most likely doomed. Finally, I could bear it no longer and cried out, "Masters. Just end it. Let my energy be destroyed."

"You'll be fine. You can do this." Henry's soothing words from so long ago appeared in my mind again, but they comforted me only briefly. What if Julianne was going to wreak her revenge now? If so, then the mission was doomed, and perhaps I would be doomed too. Could Jared have been right? Could my salvation depend on my success? Why hadn't the masters been honest about that? Did Lucio and Serene know?

Now I felt angry at everyone, and with it came a pure hatred against Jared. I wanted to hurt him, not only for what he had done to me physically, but for what he had made me feel again. I needed help, and I knew I had no choice—I would have to summon Magellan again. What would they all think?

But just as I got ready to concentrate, Lucio walked into the shop.

CHAPTER 42

Lucio looked around, searching for me and Serene. I called out to him, not caring if a live human heard.

"What happened?" he asked, running to the back of the store.

"I'm trapped."

"What? Can you move at all?"

"No! Jared was here. He sold Julianne another stone, and he did this to me. You have to free me."

"Okay, okay, let me think," Lucio said. As the moments passed in silence, I noticed Lucio looked as miserable as I felt.

"Damn it," he muttered. "We may have to contact Leonardo. I hate doing that. I've never had to do that on an assignment. But I've never run across this before."

Then, before Lucio had to resort to calling for help, the energy around me began to dissipate. Like slow-dying embers on hot wood, it disappeared, and I fell unceremoniously to the ground.

"Are you all right?" Lucio asked, helping me up.

"Yes," I said, feeling foolish and still very angry.

"Now what the hell happened, and where is Serene?" he asked, finally noticing she was gone.

"Where indeed! She's been gone for a few days now. She was upset when you didn't return. And where were you? I needed you here. People can see Jared. He met with Julianne."

"Wow," responded Lucio, stepping back to take in the news. "How is that even possible? How can he be seen?"

"It must have to do with the stones," I answered.

"It doesn't make sense."

I thought about it for a moment. Then the answer came to me clearly. Jared was, after all, an aberration. His ability to stay in live form for so long wasn't natural. Perhaps the actions of the people he sold the stones to somehow gave him power. Because Jared was now fallen, those actions would have to be evil. After all, he had pressed Julianne to go through with killing David. Who knew what other clients he had, who else he was encouraging into evil acts.

I shared my thoughts with Lucio.

"Maybe you're right," he said. "We need to act fast. You have no idea where Serene is?"

"No. I haven't looked for her. But we don't have much time. Julianne now has another stone in her possession, and Jared encouraged her to get her revenge. He kept telling her she had to do what they had discussed. We need to act before she hurts David."

"I was with her yesterday. I can call her, stall her. In the meantime, we have to find Serene. The masters put us together for a reason. She's vital to the success of this assignment too."

CHAPTER 43

We stepped out into the mall, which once again was overflowing with humanity. I figured our efforts would be useless. Serene could be anywhere. She might have even left the mall. But I needn't have worried, for Lucio understood Serene. "I think I know where she would go," he said. "Follow me."

So we walked and walked, and I realized that this mall was even more massive than I had imagined when we first walked through it. "For Serene it's either words or nature that drive her," Lucio explained. "I figure we'll start here at a bookstore, and if we can't find her, we'll go to the beach or a park."

"That will take too long," I protested.

"Well, we don't have a choice."

Books-A-Million was the mall's only bookstore, and moments after entering it, I saw that Lucio's intuition was right. There was Serene, in the store's café, in a booth with three teenage girls, discussing a school assignment, most likely. Lucio and I stood back to observe the scene. The three girls each held a copy of a book titled *A Separate Peace*. I was unfamiliar with it, but the girls' discussion was intense. "I can't stand Gene because of his jealousy," said one.

"He's hateful, and what he does is unforgivable," said another.

Then Serene joined in. "No, it's Phineas who's pushy, and worse, unaware of the effects of that pushiness," she said. "He's just as responsible for what happens."

No one, of course, heard her, and she looked away irritably. She caught sight of us then and gave us a half grin. "So you finally made it," she called out.

"Serene, next time you decide to disappear, you need to let us know where you're going," Lucio said. Then, perhaps realizing how foolish the admonishment sounded coming from one who had committed the same sin, he quickly added, "And ditto to me too. We both endangered Nicolas and almost blew our assignment."

"Is everything okay?" she asked.

"Yes, but we need to stay together now. We'll catch you up on the way out. What have you been doing for the past few days?" Lucio asked her. "Why would you run out on Nic? We talked about this."

"About what?" I interjected, but they ignored me.

"I could ask you the same," she snapped back. "What were you doing?"

He glared back at her. "I was trying to get information from Julianne. To do the assignment," he said stonily.

"To do it all right. To do her."

Lucio was silent, seeming to ignore her attempts to anger him. She turned her attention to me just as I was thinking I needed to leave them alone.

"At first I went to the poetry and philosophy section to enjoy some Thoreau and Baudelaire, but then I got bored and decided to sit with some live ones," she said, motioning to her tablemates, who had somehow switched their conversation from Gene in *A Separate Peace* to someone named Jeanine on their volleyball team. They were still oblivious to our presence.

"So they're still teaching that book. Some things never change. When we discussed Gene and Phineas's relationship in my English class, it was the same—everyone slamming Gene's flawed jealousy and speaking flatteringly about the perfect Phineas, but the truth is, Phinny was far from perfect."

"I never read the book," Lucio said.

"I never heard of it." I barely whispered my reply, worried that the girls, even caught up in their own conversation, would hear me.

"Well you should. It's really quite good. No, nothing changes, but at least sitting with those girls, I didn't feel so lonely," she said, staring at Lucio.

"We need to talk," he said.

Serene stood up and slid past the girls, who had never even known she was sitting with them. She and Lucio stared at each other. I felt uncomfortable, thinking perhaps this was a conversation they would do better alone.

"I'll just wait for you outside," I said, walking away.

"No," yelled Lucio. "We all stick together now."

They followed me out, and we sat on some benches near a fountain.

"Serene, I like you, but not enough to be your boyfriend. There, I've said it. Can you continue to work with me, or should I summon Leonardo and tell him we failed here? Cause we have to be able to work together if we're going to free the angels."

I could see the pain and anger in Serene's eyes, and I wondered why Lucio had been so blunt, so ungentlemanly.

"Why didn't you tell me before? Why did you kiss me then?"

"You're a beautiful girl, but ultimately I just see you more as a friend."

She was silent then.

"So, I guess I'll call for Leonardo," Lucio continued, sounding very disappointed.

"No, hell no, don't do that. We'll finish the damn assignment. Let's get it over with."

"Okay, and what about you, Nic? Any comments or questions here from you? Just lay it out."

I did have one question that was bothering me from my encounter with Jared. "Is it true that if I fail here, I might be sent away from the Realm? Jared told me that. Did you know that? Is that true?"

"He saw Jared?" Serene interjected.

"Yes, and we'll catch you up in a bit. But yes, Nic. That's what the rumors are, but we don't know for sure if it's true. Serene and I just didn't want to add any more pressure to this assignment. You know that there's always a test, a price, to make amends."

"Is that why you want to stay to make this work, Serene? Because you're worried about me?"

"Yes, partly. But I, like Lucio, also like to succeed. And to let those old guys and gals on the Council know I am worthy. Now I'm going to say this to you, Lucio, and you can take it as my jealousy speaking, but I hope you take it as a warning. You're the one who's putting this assignment at risk, by possibly falling in love with someone who's alive. You know you can't stay on Earth with a human."

"You're right. But I don't see how else to do it now. It gives us an advantage we might not otherwise have."

"I agree with Serene. Be careful," I said. "Jared's choice led to his fall, and I fell too. You don't know what it's like. Don't risk it. I was a shade, almost like a demon, for so long, and Jared is barely human. He's repulsive."

In my mind, I remembered how I had been, some dark, monstrous spirit, haunting poor Henry until he lost his sanity. Remembered how I'd stood behind him, whispering in his ear during their dinner one night: "You let me die. You let me die. You let me die."

I had continued my horrible chanting in his ear until he looked as if he was about to be ill. By then everyone at the table was staring at him.

"Excuse me," he said, rising quickly and dropping his napkin.

As he rushed from the room, I followed, whispering, "You let me die. You let me die." He ran upstairs into his room, and I followed as he slammed the door and flung himself on his bed. He was sweating and pale, and I was driving him to his death.

I felt tears rush into my eyes.

"Nicolas, what is it?"

Lucio's voice brought me back to the present. He was staring at me.

"I was just remembering some of the horrors of my fall. I beg of you, Lucio. Please, don't allow yourself to fall."

"I'm not going to fall," Lucio said.

I shook my head at his denial. "All it takes is one wrong decision," I said. "Look at me. Look at Jared."

"Hell. You're right," he admitted. "I don't know what I'm thinking."

We were quiet for a minute, and then Lucio started to talk.

"I guess it's just that, like you, I died young. And Julianne is hurting and is so beautiful, she's cast a spell on me. I can't control myself when I'm around her. But being with her hasn't been a waste of time. I found out where her home is—the home she's not staying at. I went there today, alone, and now I understand why she's not living there. There's an unhealthy aura about the house. It's unnaturally cold and dark, and the aura of pain and suffering from the angels is overwhelming. It's creepy."

"Did you try to break in?" Selene asked.

"Doing that in live form could be dangerous. Someone could call the police, and if I was caught, it would be a real mess. Plus, there'd be no point in me going in there now. Nothing will change until I get her to hand me the stones. It's the only way to release them. That's why continuing to go out with her is important. I'm supposed to have dinner again with her tonight."

I looked at Lucio. "So, what do you want us to do? Are you going to continue meeting with her alone?"

"No. Maybe that's not a good idea. We should go together."

We walked out of the mall, silently, and headed towards Lucio's meeting with Julianne.

CHAPTER 44

Two hours later, Serene and I sat watching Lucio and Julianne engage in an intense discussion fueled by alcohol and lies. After Lucio called her, Julianne asked him to meet her at an outdoor pub of sorts, a place called the Mai Tai, which was on the Fort Lauderdale strip, near the place we had followed her to days ago.

It was a lively place decorated with a South Pacific touch—fake coconut palms and lit torches complemented the flower-decorated drinks the waitresses brought to the patrons. We all expected that David and his band would be there and that we would have to save him from Julianne's final revenge. But there was no band playing, only recorded music, and Julianne, who had drunk three large white-colored drinks, was painfully inebriated, her speech slightly slurred and her eyes bloodshot. Still, she looked pretty and young, much younger than I knew she was.

"I wonder what that drink tastes like. That's another thing I missed out on by dying so young. I mean, I snuck some beers here and there, but I hadn't really tasted a lot of other drinks," Serene suddenly said.

Alcohol was not served in the Realm.

"In my experience, alcohol can be bad," I said. "It made Henry do things on the ship that I think he must have regretted. I don't think he would have had a relationship with Thompson if it wasn't for all that rum. After seeing what it did to Henry, I stayed away from it."

"Well, it looks kind of fun to me," said Serene, looking over at Julianne and Lucio.

"You, my dear," said Julianne, poking Lucio in the chest, "have everything."

"What do you mean," Lucio said, grabbing her hand.

"You have youth. You have passion. You have years ahead of you. Everything."

Lucio smirked, and I knew what he was thinking. He was, after all, dead. "You seemed to enjoy some passion the other night," responded Lucio, who seemed to have forgotten that Serene and I were there. I looked over at Serene as a hint of tears appeared in her eyes.

"I don't want to hear this," she said.

I didn't know what to say.

"It's all a lie," Julianne said. "Us being together is a farce. None of this is real. I'm not what I seem."

"She's right about that," Serene said.

"Then tell me what is real," Lucio said.

"I wish I could, but you wouldn't believe me."

"Try me," he said, handing her yet another drink that the waitress had just brought over.

"He's going to make her sick," said Serene.

"Yes, but for a purpose," I responded. "Remember, she has to hand the stones over of her own accord. Maybe this is his way to accomplish that."

"It's not going to work."

"Why do you say that?" I asked.

"Just a gut feeling I have."

It turned out that Serene was right. Lucio himself was beginning to become affected by the alcohol, and before we knew it, they were both oblivious to everyone around them, including us. Julianne learned towards Lucio, and he kissed her, a long, passionate kiss. It was more than Serene could bear.

"I'm outta here," she said, heading towards the door. I wouldn't let her disappear again, so I left too. She made her way out of the Mai Tai and onto the sidewalk, which was beginning to get crowded with Friday night revelers. For a while, we walked silently. I knew she was heartbroken and that there was nothing I could say to make her feel better.

"I don't know about this assignment," she finally said. "Don't you wonder why we were even sent here? It seems like we're not making any progress. Only Lucio's sex life seems to be getting that."

She looked over at me and I laughed uncomfortably.

"What do we do now?" she said. "I don't want to go watch them swap spit."

"Well, my gut, as you would put it, tells me that we need to keep an eye on David. Do you want to walk over to the place where Lucio and I first saw him and his band? Perhaps he's there again. It's not far from here. This area looks familiar."

"Sure."

After ten minutes of walking up and down several different streets, we finally walked right up to Nick's, where earsplittingly loud music spilled out onto the sidewalk. I recognized it. "That's them," I said to Serene. "Looks like they're here tonight."

We wandered in and headed to the outdoor patio area, and sure enough, Blind Passion was playing. The band was putting on quite the show, and a larger group than last time was gathered near the stage; many people were dancing. David was a charismatic performer. He had a strong voice, and although his movements seemed jerky and wild to me, his animal-like persona seemed to attract many of the young women in the crowd, who stared at him hungrily.

"Not bad," said Serene. "They're good."

So we watched. Then the band changed the pace of the performance with a slow, ballad-like tune, and many of the patrons began dancing in couples, like they were hugging each other. Very close. I'd never seen anything like it. Serene suddenly looked sad again.

"Are you fine?" I asked.

"I guess," Serene responded.

"You really love Lucio?" I asked.

"Yes. I really fell for him, but I guess he doesn't feel as strongly as I do. Not enough, anyway, to just want to be with me."

"I'm sorry."

"Well, it happens. It's just . . ."

"What?"

"I shared a lot with him, all these months. I'm going to miss that. Someone to recite my words to, someone to read poetry to."

"I'd be happy to oblige," I said.

"Okay. Here's something I wrote the other night when I ran away. Tell me what you think:

> *You are mortar and brick, foundation, support,*
> *She is wind, a rush, a flower.*
> *You are reason and sense,*
> *She's a mystery, adventure.*
> *You're a hero leading through city streets,*
> *She's still lost in the wilderness.*
> *You're my steady love,*
> *She's a flaming spark.*
> *You*
> *have been my time,*

> *She*
>
> *your greatest temptation.*
> *We three have danced this dance before, in other*
>   *times I'm sure.*

"It's lovely," I said. "It's about you, Lucio, and Julianne."

"Pretty obvious, huh," she said, laughing. "But can you do one more favor for me tonight?"

"Sure," I answered.

"Dance with me. I so miss that."

I didn't want to disappoint her, so I agreed to dance. We swayed invisibly, two angels in the center of a sea of couples. I really didn't know what I was doing; I hadn't had many opportunities to dance in my life. So I just mimicked what I saw the others around me do. It wasn't hard. Basically they just draped their arms around each other and moved slowly to the ballad. The dances from my lifetime seemed much more choreographed and less close in contact. Not being the most physical of beings, I was stiff, and somewhat uncomfortable. Serene, though, seemed to be enjoying it. She started staring into my face.

"You know, you're not half-bad looking, Nicolas. You have such beautiful eyes. Your hair could use some modernizing though. I can't believe you didn't have a girlfriend when you were alive."

"I didn't," I said stiffly.

"You didn't even ever kiss a girl?" she asked. I didn't want to tell her the embarrassing truth.

"Surely you did. Don't tell me you didn't. Well, I'll teach you," she said, moving her face towards mine.

I stepped back, much to her dismay.

"Figures," she said angrily. How could I tell her that I didn't feel attracted to her? I didn't want her, like I knew Lucio wanted Julianne. There was only one person I had ever felt that way towards, and it had been shameful and wrong.

"So what do we do now?" Serene asked grumpily after the band finished playing for the night. "Lucio and Julianne didn't show up."

"Yes, but she has another stone. I think something is going to happen. We need to be with David," I said.

"You mean follow him?" she asked.

"Yes. For now let's watch over him, be his guardian angels."

The words felt good after I'd said them. I was finally taking control of the assignment.

CHAPTER 45

Three days later, we were still watching over David. We had lost contact with Lucio again, and although I was worried about him, I knew we had to stay with David. I also knew sometimes when Serene was thinking of Lucio, as a sort of sadness would appear on her face. Still, she seemed unwilling to bring up the subject, so we just pretended that nothing at all was odd about our team leader's disappearance.

We focused on David. We'd followed him to his apartment that first night and began shadowing him as he went through his daily routines. Along with being a musician, David was also a student and spent much of his time either in classes or doing schoolwork.

It had been so long since I'd been a student, and once again I found myself in awe of the changes I saw on Earth. The rudimentary chalk and blackboard of my time was now replaced by a giant white screen from which all types of images were displayed while the masters lectured. The classes were a mix of girls and boys, and they addressed their masters more informally than we ever would have.

David's life was good, and on most days, he seemed content. But one night was different. After finishing reading in his textbooks, he suddenly became morose, just sitting silently in a chair and staring glumly into the air. He then rose from the chair and headed towards his computer. Tapping on some keys, he opened up what seemed to be a file of pictures that he clicked through.

They were all photographs of Blind Passion.

The pictures showed the band performing on various stages, and there were close-up shots of the different members at different places—the beach, various homes, outdoors. One of the people in the photos was not one of the current band members: a young man with long curly hair, sometimes playing a guitar, other times standing by his bandmates in different places. While the other band members were often laughing and smiling in the pictures, this person always appeared very serious, his eyes distant, sometimes dark.

It took me a moment, but then I realized I was looking at Harry, Julianne's now-dead son. A whisper from David broke the silence. "I'm sorry," he said. "I'm sorry."

With a click, the picture disappeared, and David pushed himself away from the computer and went off to bed, while Serene and I just looked at each other.

The next day, David seemed happier. He and several of his classmates went to the beach, with Serene and me in tow. It was the first time since our return to Earth that Serene seemed truly happy, as she ran in and out of the very strong waves that crashed along the shore. I too felt wonderful. The colors, the smell, the air, reminded me of so long ago.

"This reminds me of home," Serene suddenly said. "My family would vacation at the beach every year. It feels wonderful."

Then she surprised me when she scooped up and splashed some water, which to the observers on the beach must have looked like the spray left by a fish trying to escape the jaws of a larger one. Later, when she had come out from the waves, I saw her pick something up from the sand and stare at it.

"What is it you have there?" I asked.

"Surely you've seen this," she said, holding up what I recognized as a sea bean. I wondered if anyone on the beach was staring at what must look like a floating brown seed. "I used to love collecting these when I was alive. I do miss them. I miss everything."

I could tell she was reminiscing about her family.

"Have you gone to see your family?" I asked her.

"No, it's too dangerous. I fear it might cause me trouble, and I've been able, as hard as it is, to fight the temptation."

I so wanted to ask her more about her family, but I held back, realizing that perhaps I shouldn't even have brought them to the conversation. Live family, friends, and lovers were all a weakness for appointed angels. I of all people should know that.

Serene seemed to concur and went back to talking about the sea bean. "What's amazing about them is that they've traveled hundreds, maybe even thousands of miles from some other place just to wash up on this shore, like some adventurous travelers."

"Like us," I said.

Suddenly a roar came from the water, and I jumped. I didn't know if I would ever get used to the noises of modern life. Boats, which had once gracefully glided over waves, now ripped through the foam, powered by noisy engines.

So the day progressed. Serene continued to interact with nature, while I enjoyed watching the people: children making sandcastles, an activity that had also been popular in my lifetime; girls sunning in tiny bathing attire; and young men throwing cylinder-shaped balls to each other. David joined his friends in the water and then on the sand, and it was an enjoyable day for all—the living and dead alike.

For the first time during this assignment, I felt at home. After all, water and waves were my talent, and as if to verify my feelings, it wasn't long until I was needed. Out in the water, a boy who looked to be about twelve started yelling, and I, along with everyone else, looked over to where he was. He had his arm outstretched, pointing to another boy, who was much farther out in the water and seemed to be in trouble.

The boy was slipping under the waves, his head just peeking up over the water. I didn't take any time to think. My instincts took over, and I decided I would save that boy, orders from the Realm or not. I was still angry about not being told just how vital my success on assignment was.

Then, just as I was about to push the boy up above the waves, a live human arrived. He was a rescue swimmer of some sort, who grabbed the boy and began paddling with him back to shore. When I got back, Serene was waiting.

"Wow. I saw you go. Did you get an order?"

"No. Can they do that on the spur of the moment?"

"The masters will sometimes contact angels in the middle of an assignment. You hear their voice telling you what to do."

"Well, I decided on my own. Do you think that's going to be a problem?"

"I don't know, but he was obviously going to survive either way, so they probably won't care. But it was a risk, Nic, because you shouldn't interfere with the master plan. Sometimes bad things happen for a reason, and if you interfere, you'll be called before the Council and might be punished."

I felt scared suddenly, my bravado disappearing as I realized how reckless my actions had been. What if I had interfered and found myself once again exiled from the Realm?

"Hey," said Serene, who must have noticed the despair on my face. "You know doing something good won't lead you to fall. You know that, right? They would just talk to you or something."

"I guess," I said. I didn't feel sure of anything.

And so ended our day on the beach. We still didn't know where Lucio was, but as far as we were concerned, it no longer mattered. I sensed that things were somehow playing out as they should, and that Serene and I were meant to stay exactly where we were. Although we didn't discuss it, I thought she sensed it too. Our purpose hung over us, enveloping us like a comforting quilt.

The next day, a storm of great proportions hit Fort Lauderdale. Its ferocity reminded me of several nor'easters I'd gone through when I was alive. Blinding torrents of rain alternated with loud, booming thunder, lightning strikes, and howling winds. David glanced worriedly out his window as he talked on his cell phone.

"This weather sucks. Are you sure they still want us to play tonight? . . . You're kidding me. They want us there that early? . . . Well, as long as they pay us. I guess we can run through two performances. . . . Okay. I'll see you there around seven." Several hours later, the storm, while not totally gone, had abated, and David and his bandmates were heading again to Nick's.

CHAPTER 46

David had been right about the weather. Nick's was pretty empty when they played their "gig," as Serene called it. Only a smattering of couples and friends had made it to the tavern, but modern humanity still held a fascination for me, and I found myself staring at and analyzing the relationships between the people at the tables. There was one table with three people: a couple that held hands and another girl, who seemed to be a good friend of the female half of the couple.

At the table next to them sat two young men deep in conversation. They stared intently at each other as they spoke, and there was a deep contentment about them. It reminded me of Henry, and my thoughts returned to an afternoon long, long ago—a dreary, snowy afternoon, but Henry and I had met at his house and spent hours together just talking and laughing and scheming, and that look, that look in the men's faces, well, it was the same look that Henry had had while he talked to me, and I wondered what my own face had reflected.

Then one of the men put his hand over the other's hand. That shocked me. Why would two men display such affections in public? Weren't they worried what others would say and do?

But surprisingly, no one seemed to be minding them; only me with my thoughts of Henry.

Henry who had held my hand when I was ill. Henry whose dark eyes shone with a hint of gold, who always looked especially handsome when he laughed. Henry who . . . suddenly I wanted to leave, an uncomfortable, unbidden thought entering my mind.

"Oh my," Serene said, suddenly and loudly. "Oh God. Hurry, look to the door," she said. But even before I turned, I felt him—the smothering sensation I had experienced when Julianne met with Jared at the shop.

"It's Julianne, with some strange man," Serene said. "And where the hell is Lucio?"

I saw him then, Jared in all his ghastly brilliance. Against his black suit, shirt, and tie, his pale features and red hair stood in sharp contrast. Strangely, he reminded me of a velvet-red rose.

"It's Jared," I whispered, fear spreading through my being like a rising river.

"What do we do?" Serene asked, apprehension in her voice as well. I wasn't sure. I only knew that to stay safe, we had to keep our distance, so I told Serene about what happened the last time I encountered Jared.

"Don't get too close," I said, realizing I myself didn't know what constituted "too close." Still, I knew we needed to hear what was happening. "Just follow me. Stay behind me."

Slowly, step by step, we neared the table where the two now sat. I made a wide berth around the side of the table, then swung around the back, not too close, not too far. My plan worked. Jared, deep in conversation with Julianne, didn't notice us. We needed to hear their conversation though, and fortunately David's band had still not returned to the stage. I motioned for Serene to remain quiet, and we listened.

Julianne seemed distressed. "I don't know why you insisted on tagging along, Jared," she said angrily.

"You know why. You must do what you've come to do, and I hope that my company will help."

"I'll do it. Just at my own pace. I'm not comfortable with you here."

"Yes, you will do it. But you'll do it tonight. Have you been holding the stone?"

"Yes."

"What's the problem then?" he snapped. "Fear should not be stopping you."

"Please leave," Julianne pleaded, her voice rising enough that several other patrons looked over. "Just, please leave."

"I won't leave until you do that which you must."

"Please, I beg of you, go!" she yelled. Her hands were balled into fists, and she trembled. I don't think even she knew what she was going to do next.

A man from a nearby table rose and walked over to where Julianne and Jared sat. "Look, buddy. This lady has asked you to leave twice. I think you should."

"You," snarled Jared, "are nothing here. How dare you tell me what to do."

"Do you want me to call the bouncer?" the man asked Julianne. But before Julianne could react, a well-dressed older man walked up to the table with what seemed to be a guard of sorts.

"I'm the manager of this establishment, and I'm going to have to ask you all to leave. You are causing a disruption."

"Look, this man is harassing this lady," said the gentleman who had come to Julianne's rescue.

"Is that true?" the manager asked.

Julianne, who had begun to silently cry, nodded her head.

"Sir, leave or my security officer here will escort you out."

"That won't be necessary," snarled Jared. He got up slowly, then turned to Julianne one last time. "Do what you must," he ordered.

He then turned. As he began to walk to the exit door, I realized he was coming right towards us. Then he had come too close, had noticed us, and now was staring directly at us, at me, his eyes boring into mine. I grabbed Serene's hand and began backing up. Once again I heard his words in my head.

"It's you again, Nicolas the fallen. And I see you're with another."

The word *fallen* struck at my core, and I felt myself shaking.

"Boy, you should have heeded my last warning."

He walked calmly towards us, as if he were on a stroll in a park, and as I pulled Serene back with me, he stopped moving.

"You're lucky, Nicolas. They're watching me, making sure I leave. But mark my words. Soon. Soon I'll return you to where you truly belong."

His words terrified me. Could he really get me thrown out of the Realm?

Before I could respond in any manner, he passed us and headed out the exit door. I knew I had to stop him. I had to strike before he struck. But what could I accomplish? In my angelic state, I was useless against his live physical form, unless I was in water. Then a thought came to me. Serene might be the answer, for she could manipulate nature. Perhaps she could cause an accident to happen to Jared. He was vulnerable in his human state. Serene could lift a boulder, drop a branch, do something that could hurt him. I wasted no time.

"Let's follow him," I cried out to Serene.

"But what about David?" she protested. "What if Julianne tries to kill him?"

"We must stop Jared," I said. "You're the only one who can do it." I grabbed her hand roughly and pulled her out the door and towards Jared. He was climbing into a black vehicle.

I looked around and noticed that when he backed out of the space his automobile rested in, the car would come near a thick, tall palm tree. If only Serene could manipulate the tree somehow, make it fall on his car, perhaps she could hurt him. I wasn't sure if it would work, but in his human form, surely he could physically be stopped.

"Knock the palm onto his car, Serene," I yelled out without thinking.

"What? I can't do that. Don't you remember what Gabriel told us: to keep away from Jared, to focus on the trapped angels."

"It doesn't matter. Don't you see how dangerous Jared is? We'll be giving the Realm a gift. Knock the tree down," I yelled.

"You're asking me to do something evil with my gifts. I can't," she cried.

"Damn you, Serene. Just do it. You have to do it now."

"I can't."

I swung her around forcefully and pushed her towards the palm tree, and she began crying. There was no time left to waste with this, so I left Serene behind and ran towards the car. I didn't know what I would do, but I had to stop Jared.

The minute I neared his car, I realized the recklessness of my actions. He looked at me, and I felt once again as if I were shrinking. Then the gray fog overcame me. It was dark. I was suffocating. All went black.

CHAPTER 47

I awoke, if you can call it that, in darkness. The darkness felt familiar, in a way I dreaded. Had I fallen again? Where was I? Why couldn't I move? Then, it all came rushing back to me: my reckless pursuit of Jared, my feeble attempt to stop him. He had trapped me again. If only I had listened to Serene's advice—to stick to the assignment.

It was too late now. I wondered where Serene was and if she would be able to summon help, but as the minutes passed and the darkness of my entrapment intensified, my fears worsened. Maybe I had fallen again; after all, I felt just as I had then— invisible, a void. Maybe this was where I would remain forever.

Then the worst thought engulfed me. Henry. I knew now that I would never see Henry again. But along with the sadness at this realization came a fury. This was all his fault in the first place. *How could you, Henry? How could you betray me?* It was the question I had asked for over a century, and now, just when I had behaved so badly myself, it haunted me again, as it probably would forever.

CHAPTER 48

Piercing red eyes stared at me, like the flames of an eternal damnation. Jared was truly evil. Had I had such eyes during all those years I was fallen? Had I been that frightening? I thought of the people who had felt my presence or heard me through the years I had haunted Henry's home. Some had fled the room immediately. One child screamed when she entered the room, another cried. Had any of them seen me? Had I, in my revenge on Henry, become a grotesque demon like the one who now stood before me?

"No," I muttered to myself.

"Silly boy, I told you I'd bring you to where you belong. Did you really believe you belonged in the Realm again? They don't trust you; they don't want you, and you don't belong there."

"Liar," I said, hoping I was right.

"It's happened already. Serene told Leonardo of your choice to chase me, and they have moved on."

"I don't believe you," I whispered.

"You're a fool, Nicolas—a fool who belongs to me now. Doesn't it anger you that they left you trapped for over a hundred years? That they couldn't understand: you were just a boy."

"How do you know all this?"

"I have my sources."

Had my tome been seen by anyone other than Leonardo? Magellan said it had not, and I couldn't believe that Magellan would lie to me. Would he?

"Doesn't it anger you that, in a sense, you will always work for them? Aren't you weary of their assignments, their timetables, their wishes? Doesn't that anger you?"

"Please stop!" I yelled.

"You might as well join me. Like me, you can have a physical body again. Like me, you can be alive again, and not have to wait for someone else's decision about your rebirth—a rebirth that gives them all the power over who you'll be and where you'll go. No, I offer you a chance to be reborn as you are now: a handsome young man. Join me, and I can give you the power to make things happen how you want."

I was silent. The scenario Jared painted was very tempting. Perhaps he was right. Perhaps the only way I would see Henry again was through my own volition. The masters had made me wait, had given me no answers to the pain that plagued me, and now, trapped here, perhaps none of that mattered. I had, after all, failed to follow the assignment orders. Perhaps I had lost my chance to stay in the Realm forever.

"Yes, boy," Jared said, reading my expression. "You know I'm right. Now I'll take your hand and release you, and we'll work together."

He lifted his skeletal hand towards me, and I winced at the sight of his dagger-like nails. As I stared at his pale grotesqueness, I felt as if lightning had struck me. I knew that he was the last entity in the universe I would ever want to team up with . . . yet I so wanted to be with Henry again. If this was the only way, I would risk my eternal soul for it.

CHAPTER 49

The next morning, I sat and watched Jared eat tiny brown nuggets that came out of a box. He had spent the morning interrogating me, and I had answered his questions truthfully. I told him about our assignment, about Lucio and Serene. I told him what we'd been told about the situation in the Realm. What they believed. I was afraid of him, and I didn't know what he already knew, so I thought it better to tell the truth.

"So I've told you what I was sent for," I said. "I've told you about the team I was on, about our assignment, about what they know about you. I've answered your questions. So you, Jared, must tell me something. How are you in this live state?"

We were sitting around a small rectangular table in what seemed to be the drawing room of his rather small canal-front home. Everything about Jared's place was dark and bare and cold. A few chairs littered the room we were in, and that was all. Black curtains kept out the bright Florida sun, and as I sat there, I noticed a rat scurrying across the floor. This was no home; it reminded me of a vampire's tomb.

"Patience, boy, patience. Eventually you'll understand how everything works, but for now you must do what I say."

"What do I have to do?"

"First you must help me finish the job with Julianne. Once that is done, once her actions are complete, I will see about you. You can join us and eventually be like me."

"What do you want me to do?" I repeated.

"Keep Serene and Lucio away from me and Julianne," he said. "Distract them so they don't interfere. Can you do that, boy?"

"Yes," I said. "Except I don't know where they are."

"Believe me, they'll appear again. After all, Julianne is your assignment, isn't she?"

"Yes."

"Tomorrow Julianne will complete her part in all this, but until then, until you can prove yourself to me through your actions, I must insist on imprisoning you."

"It's not necessary," I complained, but before I could continue, I found myself stuck again, unable to control my movement. "Please," I cried. "I promise I won't go anywhere. At least let me be comfortable."

"Fine," he said, releasing me. "Follow me."

I knew I had no choice. He locked me in an empty room in his small home. I could move about, but I could not open the door or the window. In one corner of the room was a pillow and some blankets. The hours dragged by interminably till evening. When night came, I made myself a makeshift bed. It reminded me of my time aboard the *Mary Selina*, when Henry and I shared the cramped space of the forecastle.

At first, sleep did not come; instead, I contemplated my circumstances. I wondered about Serene and Lucio. Where were they? What were they thinking of me? What were they doing? Could I really betray them for Henry? Thankfully, these thoughts did not torture me for much longer until I fell into an uneasy slumber.

I awoke, and it was still dark out. I wasn't sure how long I had been asleep, but there was a light coming through the bottom of the door of the room I was in. Lights were obviously on in another part of the home. Then I saw a shadow pass, breaking the light that streamed through the crack under the door, and I heard voices. Jared was not alone. What was happening?

I crawled on my hands and knees towards the door, careful to make no sound. I got as close as I could to the gap at the bottom of the door and listened.

"Ten more. That's wonderful, but are you sure you're being careful enough?" I heard Jared say.

"Gabriel and the others are too trusting," said a soft, musical voice.

I knew that voice. It sounded so familiar. "They suspect no one, least of all me. They think the traitor is someone in Irelae who has easy access to the Realm, not the opposite."

I knew then who it was. That was Allie's distinctive flute-like voice. Allie was giving the Jared the stones? How could that be? She had seemed such a sweet person.

"History has proven differently, and yet they persist in their illusions," Jared said. "The boy told me they believe I stole the stones originally for good reasons—because I could not bear to lose the child on my assignment. The simpletons, always wanting to think the best of everyone." He laughed.

"May they persist in their ignorance," the woman—Allie—said. "But I tire of the Realm. It's so dreadfully boring, and the assignments are relentless. When will it be my turn to enjoy Earth again as you are, Jared? To feel alive again."

It was hard to believe this was the same person I had seen crying at the art museum.

"It will happen, my love. It will. I want you here with me, you know that. But it will take time, and the more stones the better."

They went quiet. I wondered what was happening. I was becoming impatient by the time they started speaking again.

"Jared, I waited so long to be with you, and now we are still separated. You are tactile again, and I am all spirit."

My mouth dropped open. I couldn't believe Allison would find Jared appealing in any way. But, I realized, these two seemed to have a history. Perhaps a history like Henry and me.

"My dear," Jared said, "we've come so far, and I will not let you down. Patience. You must have patience."

"What did he tell you?"

"A death makes it permanent. For now my 'aliveness' is only temporary, but once Julianne kills the boy, he will grant me life again, and we can begin working on making it happen for you as well, as long as you follow his will."

"And what of Nicolas? What are you going to do with him?"

"If he tries to escape, I'll entrap him, but he agreed to help me, and I think he will. He's weak, too attached to his former life, and I think I can use that."

"How can he help you with this Julianne?"

"He can keep the others away."

"And José, how is he working out?"

"He is vital to this effort. After all, the humans have to come to us. It must be of their free will. I can encourage them, but they have to want it. José has been good at getting us the clients and enjoying the riches."

"So it's all working out."

"So it seems, but I want to ask you a favor. Talk to the boy, let me know what you think. Tell me if you think I should trust him tomorrow."

They stopped talking, and then I heard footsteps, heading towards me. There was a knock on the door.

"Nicolas, wake up," said Allison, and Jared opened the door for her and walked away.

CHAPTER 50

Allison walked in looking as innocent as that 1950s actress and singer Annette Funicello. Her hair was in a ponytail, and she wore a pink sweater and tight black pants. I didn't know what to say to her; I was so shocked at her betrayal of everyone in the Realm. Then I realized that I was doing exactly the same and felt ashamed.

"I'm glad you're joining our side, Nicolas," she said. "You are, aren't you?"

"Yes," I muttered.

"It's for your friend. Henry? Right?"

"How do you know? Who told you about Henry? Did you read my tome?"

"None of that matters. There are ways to get information in the Realm. Let's just say it's a more complicated place than some know. But you're doing the right thing joining us. I understand your frustration with the Council. I'm tired of waiting on them to let me reunite with my love. It's been over sixty years now."

"What are you talking about? Was Jared your love on earth?"

She smirked. "He's not who I'm talking about," she whispered. "Although that's what I want him to think. He's a means to my end. My true love has been reborn and is here on Earth now. I want to be able to find him as a live person. Jared was my only chance of making that happen, so I've let him believe that he's the one I'm doing this for. He's always liked me."

"But how do you know your true love will even know you? He's a different person now."

"He's my soul mate, and so we will reunite."

"And you've been waiting for over sixty years? I can't wait that long to see Henry."

"Then you've made the right choice. You're doing the right thing," she said, and she turned from me and walked out the door, closing it behind her.

"Wait," I called after her. It was useless. She was gone.

I fell back onto my makeshift bed, but this time sleep would not come.

Was I doing the right thing? How could I do this to Lucio and Serene? Lucio had been right about me; I was bringing failure to the assignment. But why? Why was I allowing myself to do this?

It finally came to me: it was fear. Fear can cause us to do the worst of actions. Fear can lead us to Hell. It was fear that had kept Henry from admitting to his wrongdoing, fear that led him to allow me to pay for his grand sin. It was fear that made me chase Jared when I should have stayed with Serene and David. And that led me to work with the enemies of the Realm.

Suddenly, after so long, I understood how Henry must have felt: terrified that his actions, that accidental murder, would lead to his own demise.

"I forgive you, Henry," I whispered in the darkness.

CHAPTER 51

Morning came in the form of another wet South Florida squall. Jared skipped breakfast and stayed in his bedroom, where he ignored me the rest of the day, which dragged on in gloom and humidity. Eventually I found myself watching television, getting caught up in an all-day news channel.

The drama of the modern world was overwhelming. The world had always been a violent, often scary place, but modern technologies made it all too much. Modern-day humans were constantly bombarded with horrors that occurred thousands of miles away and barely affected them. Did they really need to know everything bad that was happening everywhere? It made me sad.

Finally, around seven o'clock, Jared exited his room. He was dressed as a gentleman, in a dress shirt, tie, and pants. "It's time to meet Julianne," he said. "Remember your assignment. If Serene and Lucio show up, you run to them and distract them. Do not let them interfere."

"Yes," I said, feeling very bad about this.

"This time we'll stay with her until she does what I've ordered," he said. "I think my encouragement has strengthened

Julianne's resolve to get revenge, and another visit will do the trick. I'm bringing you along, but I'm warning you, boy, don't cross me. If you do, you will never be safe, no matter where you are."

CHAPTER 52

We began our ride in a tempestuous Florida storm; we ended it in drizzle. Tiny drops splattered the windshield as Jared pulled into the parking lot of a gasoline station. There, under the waning light of a dim streetlamp, stood Julianne, wet and wide-eyed.

"Thanks for coming, my dear," Jared said, smooth as silk, as Julianne opened the passenger door beside him. "They're playing at Nick's again tonight. It's time this story comes to its needed conclusion."

"I wish I had never met José, or you," Julianne said, standing with her hand on the vehicle door.

"Really, my dear? Really? Look at yourself. Not only are you beautiful, but you will now do what you have so longed to do."

"That's true, but I am still conflicted."

"Once you do it, your conflict will end."

"You're right. Of course you're right." Still, she hesitated.

"Now, my dear, you know you've been wanting to do this for so long. Think of your son, your poor young innocent boy, who will never be on this Earth again thanks to the actions of David."

His words woke her as if from a sleep, and she quickly entered the car. The storm outside may have ended, but the front had arrived.

CHAPTER 53

We sat at a table while Blind Passion performed. I had looked to see if Serene or Lucio were around, but I hadn't seen them. What had happened to them? Why weren't they here? I saw Jared lean over to say something to Julianne, but because of the loud music, I couldn't hear what he said. Then he put his hand into his pocket and pulled out his car keys. He handed them to Julianne, who rose.

"What's happening?" I yelled over to Jared.

"Get in front of her now, and stop Serene and Lucio if you see them outside. I'll stay here and enjoy David's music. After all, it's the last time he'll ever perform."

I shivered at his evil, talking about a young man's death with such calm. As I walked out with Julianne, I scanned the parking area and sidewalk around the club, happy that Serene and Lucio were nowhere to be seen. There wasn't much I could do to stop any of it anyway. I felt like a moth ensnared in a spider's web.

I watched as Julianne opened, then entered, Jared's car. For a few minutes, she just sat there, and then she reached down for something—a scarf that she tied over her head. She started the car and slowly drove it out towards the road in front of the bar. Suddenly a group of people came from behind me and walked on by. One of them was David; the band must have stopped playing.

As David walked past me, I watched him take out a package of cigarettes from his pocket and pull one out. He headed towards a tall palm tree that bordered the parking area. Suddenly there was a loud squeal and a thumping noise, and I looked towards the sound to see Jared's car coming up off the street, towards the tavern, straight towards David. I heard a cacophony of cries, but David seemed to be frozen in place, a look of shocked surprise on his face. I too found myself unable to react. Then I heard her.

"Nic, Nic, Julianne's going to run him over!" Serene screamed. "I don't know how you got here, but what do we do?" I looked over, surprised.

"She's going to murder him!" she screamed.

Murder.

The word snapped me to my senses. I had been brutally murdered. There was no way I was going to be part of this young man's murder. There was no way I was going to cross Serene, Lucio, and everyone I knew in the Realm. If I had to wait sixty years to see Henry, then I would wait. I would not fall into the darkness by being part of someone else's murder.

"The tree, Serene. Use the tree. Create a barrier," I yelled at her. Serene jumped into action, heading not towards David, but rather towards the large palm tree near him. Then she disappeared into the tree, and the tree swayed violently, bending down in a most peculiar fashion, almost as if it was bowing. As David stumbled back, away from the oncoming car, the car ran into the tree first, which somewhat slowed its forward motion, but David was still struck by a part of the tree the car pushed forward, splintered where it had bent. As people rushed towards the scene, Julianne reversed the damaged vehicle, and I saw Jared rush up to the car and jump in before the car backed onto the road and sped off.

Serene suddenly reappeared and ran to David.

"Follow them," she yelled at me. "I'll stay here with him. We still need the stones." I ran off then, down the road, only to see the black car turn right onto another road. I kept running, but the car was too fast, and I lost them.

What a mess, I thought, helplessly. We had all really failed this assignment.

In the distance, I could hear the strange wailing noise of modern emergency vehicles, and I knew that police and medical care had been dispatched. I hoped somehow David had survived. Just as I was about to turn back towards Nick's, I noticed someone walking quickly down the sidewalk far ahead of me. She looked petite and blond and carried a really large purse. Could it be Julianne? Had Jared dropped her off and driven away? It would make sense.

I ran until I caught up with her. It was Julianne, unharmed and strangely calm. I wanted to yell at her. She had hurt David, maybe killed him. She had done what I had done—given in to the need for revenge—and like me, she would learn that revenge never led to any resolve, only more pain. I followed her as she walked and walked past busy restaurants and shops, ignoring the traffic that roared by her on the Fort Lauderdale streets. I wondered where she was going and why it was taking her so long to get there, but mostly I wondered why she was so calm after committing such an evil act. After all, her son chose to kill himself. It wasn't David's fault.

Then I realized that in a sense, it was the same with Henry. The actions of others had not been directly his fault. He had eventually told them the truth, but they hadn't believed him. He had not been the one who tossed me off the ship.

Julianne walked up to a Chinese restaurant and then stopped, pulled a tiny telephone from her large purse, and made a quick phone call. Several minutes later, a taxi pulled up, and I hopped in with her. We didn't go far. About ten minutes later, the taxi pulled into what looked to be the entrance to a shipping port.

What in the world? I thought. There was a large-gated entrance with an officer of some sort, and after several moments, the taxi was waved through. We were dropped off in front of a large concrete and glass building from which many people were entering and leaving. When we entered, I could see through gigantic clear windows that a monstrous, mammoth ship was docked behind the building. It was the largest ship I'd ever seen in person. It reminded me of a whale.

While the *Mary Selina* had looked like a bird, with its wing-like sails, this ship had a colossal broad bow, like a whale's head, and extending rails at its stern that looked like a whale's flukes. The top of the ship seemed to be layered with a series of decks, like gigantic steps. I followed Julianne as she went to the back of a winding line of people. At the front of the line, ship officials looked at paperwork that people showed them. When we finally got to the front, Julianne pulled out some paperwork from her purse; she was waved through, and I found myself with Julianne on a gangplank. Finally, after so many years and years, here I was again on the deck of a ship.

CHAPTER 54

The deck was packed with all types of people, and an excited and noisy crowd it was. There were couples—young, middling, and old—and groups of friends. Many of them already had drinks in their hands as they waited for the ship to sail. I found it odd that a ship was leaving port at such an odd hour, but this was no working ship. It was like one big festival.

As I stood there next to Julianne, Lucio suddenly appeared, working his way through the mass of people. "Where have you been?" Lucio yelled at her. "I thought you were going to miss the launch."

"I had some complications," she answered. Then Lucio glanced past Julianne, saw me, and turned pale.

I pointed away, to try to tell him we needed to talk.

"What is it?" Julianne asked, noticing Lucio's surprised look and peering back to see what he saw. She, of course, could not see me.

"Nothing. It's nothing," he said.

"Well then, let's go," Julianne said, grabbing Lucio's hand and heading towards the starboard side of the ship. I followed. I would have to wait for Lucio to decide to talk to me. Even though I had no idea if David had survived, I found myself strangely calm as the ship headed out to sea, lulled by the beauty of the rolling dark ocean and the endless sky-field of stars.

I realized then how much I had missed being aboard ship. I wished I had had more times like this and less of the strife that both Henry and I had experienced. Most of the time I had spent at sea had been drudgery, but here on this ship, the passengers seemed to be enjoying a king's life: feasting, drinking, dancing, and playing.

Julianne and Lucio seemed to enjoy it too. Standing near a railing, they were quiet, kissing each other until I began to feel uncomfortable again. After some time, I wondered if Lucio was ever going to pay any attention to me. I began waving my arms to get his attention.

He finally broke from Julianne's grasp, looked at me angrily, and announced, "I need to find a restroom. I'll be back." Julianne leaned over and gave him another big kiss and tight hug. She hung on until he finally pulled away.

"I'll be right back," he said.

We walked away to a place where no one would notice him talking to the air.

"Where have you been? Why are you here?" he blurted out.

"I should ask you the same, Lucio. But it's bad. Earlier tonight, Julianne followed David to Nick's, and when he was outside, on a break from performing, she tried to run him over. Serene was able to blunt the blow by manipulating a tree, and that may have saved his life. But I can't say for sure. Serene stayed with him, and I followed Julianne."

Lucio stepped back, looking as if he'd been punched in the belly. "I've really screwed up," he said. "She's going to be in trouble now. I don't know what's wrong with me—I shouldn't have disappeared with Julianne again. It's just . . . Well, I've told myself I would get the stones from her when the time was right.

So I've been with her most of the time, but when I returned to the mall to look for you two and you didn't return, I realized I had messed up again. You see, she surprised me with tickets to the *Sea Endeavor*—this ship—a few nights ago, and I decided that tonight would be the night I would get the stones from her. I would fess up to what I was and confront her about what she was doing. But I waited too long. I'm weak around her. I think . . . I think I've fallen in love with her. The masters will be furious. I've let them down—and worse, you and Serene, and the trapped angels. God, Nic, I don't know what to do."

"You have to confront her now. This has to end. You're in danger of doing something you'll regret. You're not alive, Lucio. If you want that, you need to ask to be reborn."

"I know," he said quietly.

"But I still don't get it," I said. "Something isn't right here. Why would she make plans for this trip on the same night she planned to kill David?"

We both looked at each other, and suddenly we knew. We ran then, Lucio dodging between groups of laughing people and heading towards where he had last left Julianne standing. As we neared, we heard a scream and the sudden frenzy of many voices. "Someone's fallen overboard!" a woman screamed.

Then all chaos seemed to break out, with crowds of people rushing towards the railings and crew members running about. A loud announcement boomed: "Bravo, Bravo, Starboard. Bravo, Bravo." I knew it was an emergency call that someone had fallen overboard.

The noise snapped Lucio and me out of our shock. I then realized Julianne's plan: she would kill David and then herself, and that's why she went on the cruise and why she needed the Bravery stone. Not to kill David, but to kill herself.

"Julianne!" I heard Lucio yell. "Save her, Nic!"

"I'll get her," I told him. And I jumped up onto the rail and overboard. *Just like old times,* I thought as I fell into the water.

CHAPTER 55

I found her quicker than I expected. She was letting herself drown, sinking below the waves. Seeing it—seeing her mimic my actions from so many eons ago—brought back all the pain and fear I had experienced. This time it shocked me into quick action. I would not let it happen again.

I dove after her, grabbed her, and with lightning quickness brought her to the surface, where she gasped and coughed up water. Meanwhile, I was struck by a brightness that at first blinded me. There was some sort of light, as bright as the sun, scanning the ocean's surface. I could hear the sound of engines again, and I saw that there were two small silver boats heading towards us.

I had to move, and quick, so I dove again, taking Julianne with me, hoping I wouldn't drown her. She was mine for now; there would be time later for the human authorities to deal with her. I swam away with Julianne, like a dolphin skimming below the water, swam and swam until I knew we were far enough away they wouldn't search here, at least not yet. When we broke the surface again, she began gasping for air.

"What are you?" she screamed hoarsely when she finally caught her breath. "What's touching me? Let me go, let me go!"

She became frantic then, thrashing wildly with her legs, her arms pinned by mine. There was no way she could overpower me, but I had to calm her.

"It's okay, Julianne," I whispered. "Don't be afraid."

"Let me go," she cried. "What are you?"

Then she wept, as I whispered to her, and like a child who cries herself to sleep, she became silent and still.

"Is this real? Am I dead already?" she asked.

"No. You're very much alive."

"What are you?" she asked again.

"An angel," I answered.

"No angel would come to me after what I just did," she yelled. "You must be a demon."

"You're wrong," I said.

"Why would an angel save me?" she muttered. "I'm not worth saving. I don't deserve to be saved. I've done something really bad."

"I know."

"Who are you?" she asked again.

"I already told you," I answered. "But I don't think you killed David, although I'm sure you hurt him."

"How do you know about that? About David?"

"Do you believe me now?" I asked her.

"I don't know. This is crazy."

"You've committed one grave act, Julianne. You can't commit another."

"How do you know my name? Do you know everything about me?" she asked.

"Only about this situation," I said.

"Then you should understand that I want to be with my son. I miss him so much," she said, starting to cry again. "Is this real?" she asked again.

"Of course."

That seemed to bring her some comfort, so I said nothing else. We both were silent in the water while I thought about what to do next. Then Julianne began to shake, the coldness of the water affecting her. I noticed then how pale she was. I had to get her out of the water, quickly, and back to the ship, so I once again dove beneath the water and swam nearer to the ship.

I had to sneak her aboard somehow, but how? Then I had it. I had read up on the evolution of ships through the decades, and had learned a little about modern ships. Many modern ships had a sea-level entrance that was used to get tugboat pilots and other officials aboard. I could enter through there, although I'd have to wait until someone opened that water-tight hatch.

I swam around the ship, carrying a now limp Julianne, and spotted the door. We were so close. But there was no way to open the door from the outside. If only I could get Lucio to open the hatch. But how?

I knew at that moment that only one person could help.

Magellan. Magellan. Magellan. I thought his name over and over, hoping that he would get here soon, before the searchers appeared and caught sight of Julianne or she died of exposure.

"Gosh darn it, boy, what is it this time? I was just relaxing in my nice warm bed with a hot cup of cocoa."

I heard his voice before I saw him, and I turned around to see a most peculiar sight: Magellan dressed in a cream-colored nightcap and gown, floating just above the waves.

"Thank God you've come," I cried. "I'm in the midst of a bit of an emergency with Julianne. I need you to find Lucio aboard the ship and somehow get him to open that hatch door over there, so I can get Julianne back inside before she succumbs to the elements. She's already unconscious."

Magellan took one look at her and said, "I'll see what I can do. And by the way, I'm glad to see that at least some of your team is back together again."

And so we waited. And waited. Then finally, when I had almost given up hope, I saw the hatch door opening, and there were both Lucio and Magellan staring at me.

CHAPTER 56

Julianne—conscious, dry, comfortable, and safe now—sat on a small bunk in the cabin she and Lucio would have shared. Wide-eyed, she stared at Lucio. "So you're like him—the voice," she said to Lucio, nervously laughing. "It makes sense that you would be an angel. You're too beautiful to be true. But then, none of this seems real anymore. I feel as if I'm in a dream."

"No, Juli, it's real," Lucio said.

"But I can see and feel you. Why not him?"

"He doesn't have the power yet. But that's beside the point. What type of life do you want to live, Juli? Has all this made you happy? Has it brought you peace? Has it brought Harry back? You must return the angel stones."

She gasped. "How do you know about the stones? How . . . ?" Then she stopped. "I suppose that would make sense," she whispered.

"You having the stones is an abomination that has lasting repercussions," Lucio admonished. "Those stones are tied in essence to angels. Angels you've now trapped in your home. You have to give me the stones in order to release them. It's the only way to make things right."

"I don't know if I can do that," she said.

"How did you get them in the first place?" I interjected. I was standing next to Lucio, and she looked over to where I was, shaking her head.

"I still can't believe any of this is true! A disembodied angel voice. This is so strange."

"It's no stranger than you looking like you're twenty-five without plastic surgery and treatments," snapped Lucio.

"Now tell us how you got the stones," I said.

"It was innocent, at first," she said. "I was so depressed about Harry, feeling so old, feeling that everything was pointless. Then I met this man named José who used to hang out at the Emporium, and he suggested I buy a stone. He said they had special powers and would help me feel better. I didn't really believe him; I just bought them on a lark, hoping that I could use them for meditation. But then something strange happened. I noticed the years fading from me, and it brought me a sort of comfort and confidence. Eventually it changed my life. I regained my looks, got a new job, a new place, but I still wasn't happy. And then my home became uninhabitable. I contacted José about the problem, and Jared showed up with him. In talking to him about what had happened, well, he somehow seemed to get into my head. You have to understand, I was still suffering the loss of Harry, and then the plan, the revenge, came to mind. At that moment, I knew there had been a purpose for me stumbling across such magic."

"What you've done is so wrong," Lucio said.

"What they did to Harry was wrong," she snapped. "Plus, I can't give the stones to you. It will change everything."

"To what it should be," Lucio said.

"No," she said angrily. "I won't give them up. They're all I have now. What do either of you know about it? You don't understand and you will never understand. David was so cruel to my son, my only child. Harry told me how David would always make fun of him and yell at him in front of the others when he felt he wasn't playing well. After he kicked Harry out of the band, it was like something permanently broke in Harry. He couldn't go on. It's David's fault that he's dead, and David had to pay."

"You're wrong, Julianne. He may have been cruel, but it wasn't your place to decide his punishment. It's not your place," Lucio said.

"What would you know about feeling like you have to kill someone?"

I laughed. "Nearly two hundred years' worth," I said. "I'm the same as you."

"But how could that be? You said you're an angel."

"Just give us the stones," Lucio demanded.

"I won't," she snapped back. "I did what I had to do, what was owed to Harry."

Lucio looked over at me, and I could see the frustration in his eyes, a mirror of my own feelings. We both knew we couldn't force her to give us the stones.

"What you did was wrong, and you will pay for it, just as I did," I said. "But perhaps in giving us the stones, your punishment won't be as bad."

"I don't care," she said.

"I know; that's how I thought I felt, but then when the person I took my revenge on killed himself . . . well, I realized that I still didn't feel any better. Do you feel better now, Julianne? Do you feel better thinking you may have killed David?"

"No, not really."

"Someone I cared for very much led me to my death, and I later haunted him until he committed suicide. So you see, Julianne, I too exacted my revenge against someone, to my everlasting regret."

"I'm sorry," she said.

My eyes filled with tears as I once again recalled what I had done to Henry.

Then suddenly I wanted to say it—to finally tell someone the truth about why I had done what I had done. The situation with Julianne seemed secondary at the moment; I needed to finally say it aloud.

"You know, Lucio, the first time I saw Henry after my death, I almost changed my mind about haunting him. I could see that he carried the weight of my death on his shoulders; his pain was so etched in his appearance. I was going to leave him in peace, but then I found out he was going to get married, and I became obsessed with punishing him. All this time, I've wanted everyone to think that I was angry just because he had gone on with his life while mine had been stolen from me because of his mistakes, but the truth is somewhat different. The truth is, I don't think I would have gone so far in my haunting except for one thing."

I stopped. Lucio waited patiently until I continued.

"You see, it wasn't just that I was angry that Henry had gone on with his life, while I was dead; it was that I feared he no longer loved me. I was jealous, jealous of Shelley Witham, because I'm . . ."

I stopped again.

"You're what?" Lucio pressed.

"I don't know if I can tell you," I said, suddenly feeling my face flush with shame.

"What is it, Nic? Tell me—you obviously need to tell someone."

"Oh, just tell him, for God's sake," Julianne interjected loudly. I had almost forgotten she was there.

"Come on," Lucio said, sounding irritated.

"Fine, fine," I said, and finally blurted out what I had kept secret for so very, very long. "I loved Henry in a way that was wrong, because we were both boys."

"Oh, I understand now. So you're gay. That's all," Lucio said quietly.

I didn't understand what he meant. I wasn't feeling happy.

"There's nothing wrong with that," Julianne said. Still I remained silent.

"Look, Nic, times have changed," Lucio said. "People have become more accepting of couples of the same sex. I'm not going to lie to you; not everyone accepts it, but it is getting better in this world, and in the Realm, it's not an issue. But even so, none of that should matter to you. If you get the chance to see Henry again, don't be ashamed of your love, because if you find real love, love that you can have, you should embrace it."

At that moment, I realized that he was right, and if I had the chance to see Henry again, I would be true to myself.

"I just hope that somewhere in this universe I get the chance," I said.

Julianne suddenly gasped. "You're so young," she said.

I looked at her, and she was staring right into my eyes. Could she see me?

"Oh my God," she said.

"You can see me?" I asked.

She bobbed her head up and down.

"How can this be?" I said.

"I don't know," said Lucio. "Maybe it's because you're not hiding from who you are anymore."

CHAPTER 57

Time passed, and the three of us still sat in the cabin. Our attention had returned to our assignment, and Lucio and I were staring at Julianne, hoping we could irritate her enough to make her want to give up the stones.

She stared back at us sullenly.

"You must give them up," Lucio said angrily. "You're hurting others who have nothing to do with Harry and David."

"We won't leave without the stones," I added. "We have all the time in the world. Even if you don't."

"This won't bring Harry back," Lucio repeated. "And you'll spend a lifetime tied to Jared. Is that what you want?"

Still nothing. The minutes ticked by. We could see the struggle in Julianne's eyes; she seemed to be internally debating what to do. Then—

"I'm so very tired," Julianne said suddenly. "I don't think I can go on with this. I'll give you the damn stones. But I'll give them only to Nic. Lucio, let's say our goodbyes now. I don't want you to see me as I was before, but to remember me like this."

"It's okay. I don't care about any of that," he pleaded.

"I won't give up the stones otherwise," she insisted. "Can you go outside the room, Nic? Can you give us a moment to say our goodbyes privately?"

I stepped out, and after about five minutes, Lucio rushed out and past me without turning around. I knew he was upset. I walked back into the cabin to a crying Julianne.

"Give them to me now, Julianne. Hand them over," I said, afraid she would change her mind. She got up and went to a nightstand, where she had laid the wet clothes she'd changed out of when we first reached the cabin. She picked up a pair of wet dungarees and, with some difficulty, forced her hand down into the pocket. Then she pulled out three clear stones.

They were smaller than the one I had seen C.J. hold. One flickered gold, the other silver, and a third brown. I brought my hand to hers and grasped them, taking them from her. Once the stones were in my hands, the change that came over Julianne was instantaneous: a youthful, beautiful woman who looked like she was in her twenties transformed into a middle-aged woman. Lines appeared on her forehead, and the skin of her chin loosened. Her body seemed to widen, and while she was still a pretty woman, she looked like she could be Lucio's or my mother.

I sat down and sighed. Our assignment was accomplished, and at that moment, I had hope that it would be enough, and that I would not be sent away from the Realm.

CHAPTER 58

I said my goodbye to Julianne, knowing that she would eventually come to task for what she had done to David. But I wasn't sure she would be held accountable in her current life. The odds were that unless she herself confessed to the authorities, Julianne wouldn't be arrested. Nobody would be able to tie her to the attack on David. After all, it wasn't her car, and even if someone had noticed her face, she no longer looked like the same woman. Even David and his friends didn't know who the pretty young woman was who always stared so angrily at David.

That young woman was gone forever in this life.

I looked down at the stones in my hand and debated what to do. I could always start meditating and go straight back to the Realm. Then again, that wouldn't be fair to Lucio and Serene, who had also been part of this mission. We should all return together, I decided. Now I just had to find them. Lucio was still somewhere aboard the ship, and I hoped Serene would be at Nick's, where I last saw her.

I left the cabin and made my way up to the deck to look for Lucio. It was harder to find him than I had imagined; the deck was chaotic and noisy, and people were packed shoulder to shoulder, many with alcoholic beverages in hand. As I walked into the mob, the most amazing thing happened. I ran straight into someone.

"Hey, watch where you're going, you idiot," a white-haired man said, and a group of young women huddled right next to me laughed. I looked over at the girls, and they were staring me in the face. They could see me! I had figured my visibility would be short-lived, or maybe only for Julianne, as a way of completing the assignment. I hadn't expected this.

I wondered if, like Lucio, I was luminous in some way. The continued stares of the girls embarrassed me, so I began pushing through the crowd, enjoying this ability to feel alive on Earth again—to be solid instead of ghostly. Minutes passed as I continued my fruitless search for Lucio. After a while, I gave up and stood at the railing, staring into the cloudless starry skies.

"There you are!"

I turned around to find Lucio standing in front of me.

"Do you have the stones?" he asked.

"Yes," I said, opening up the palm of my hand to show him.

"Thank God," he sighed. "It's over then."

"We need to get Serene and head home to the Realm," I reminded him.

"Yes, but we can't forget to check on the trapped angels. I'm not sure if they were freed the minute Julianne handed over the stones or not. I made sure when I said goodbye to her to ask her for her house key. I told her I would hide the key in the front bushes of her house when I left, but that I had to have access to her place to rescue the trapped angels. She agreed."

Lucio's eyes darkened, and I realized he was still sad about losing Julianne.

"Are you all right?" I asked. "Are you going to be okay?"

"It's hard, but like other things, I can't change it. I can't be with Julianne in this life of hers."

"Yes," I said, thinking of Henry again.

After some time passed, the ship began moving again, leaving the area where Julianne had jumped. Lucio explained that this was a "cruise to nowhere," where the ship went out just far enough offshore to let the passengers drink, dance, and gamble, and then returned home again. I found the whole concept rather odd. Still, we were trapped, in a sense. We could not get back to Serene until the ship returned to port.

"We might as well join the fun," Lucio said, heading to the bar to buy drinks.

He brought me one back, and I decided that I would try alcohol again. I set the stones in my pocket as I reached for the drink. Maybe this time I would like the taste. I coughed at its jarring harshness, remembering my taste of rum with Henry and Thompson. This time, though, I continued drinking until I felt giddy. At one point, I found myself on a dance floor with some girl who had started talking to Lucio and me. I knew I must have looked silly dancing, but the alcohol had dimmed all my sense of propriety, and the night continued in a haze of loud voices and music.

Dawn was beginning to peek above the horizon as the ship returned to port, where we would begin our long walk back to Nick's. It was still pretty dark out, and the streets were relatively empty. Heading towards us were two men. I thought they would walk around us, but instead one walked right between us, noticing nothing, and I realized that our visibility on Earth was gone again.

When we finally got to Nick's, I was pleased to see Serene loitering outside by the fallen palm tree. Immediately I sensed the tension in the air. Serene and Lucio barely acknowledged each other, looking away awkwardly. Serene's mouth was drawn tight, until she looked me in the face and smiled. "You've changed. There's something different about you."

"Yes," I answered.

Then I remembered David.

"Did David survive?" I asked.

"Yes," she answered. "He's hurt, but I believe he'll survive."

"Thank goodness," I answered.

"Now, what happened with you two? What happened to Julianne?"

"It's a long story," I said, "but look." I pulled the stones out of my pocket to show her.

"That's so great. So great," Serene said, hugging me.

I felt happier than I had in as long as I could remember, as if the web that had ensnared me for so long had been snipped. I felt free. But I noticed that Lucio had sat down on the grass and was looking sad. I sat down beside him and joined in his silent contemplation.

"Let's go, let's go. What's wrong with you two?" Serene suddenly demanded. "We still need to finish this, to free the trapped ones."

"Just give him some time," I said, interrupting Serene, and when she looked over at me, I shook my head.

Serene joined us on the grass, fuming. "The masters are not going to be happy with us. We need to be doing something to finish this, and I for one am not going to take any flak for your inaction," she complained.

"She's right," Lucio said suddenly, jumping up and shaking his head, as if trying to snap himself out of inaction. "We need to finish this. Let's go."

CHAPTER 59

We rode in a taxi again, for what would be my last ride on Earth for a long time. Lucio became visible again to call for the cab. I could not muster my visibility at will yet. Maybe the power was available if the assignment called for it. I would have to ask Leonardo more about this when we returned to the Realm.

It was a silent cab ride. Lucio and Serene still seemed unhappy with each other. We arrived at Julianne's yellow-painted house on the corner of 83rd Terrace and Palm Street in Sunrise, Florida, and it looked the same as every other house on the street—except that this was the place where angels had been trapped and now, hopefully, would finally be freed.

We didn't know what to expect. The minute we entered the house, we could hear the odd moaning. We stopped near the front door and looked at each other. "Wait here," Lucio said. "I'll check it out."

Serene and I were happy to agree to his suggestion. The moaning was becoming unbearable, reminding me of some tortured souls' laments in a horror tale.

"They're in bad shape," Lucio said, rushing back. "We need to get them back to the Realm. They seem like they're fading. Serene, contact Leonardo. Nic, come with me."

I followed Lucio towards the room where the two angels had been trapped for months. They lay still on the floor of a cluttered space filled with books, a computer, and assorted shelves of knickknacks. At first I thought we had arrived too late. The moaning had ended abruptly, and their skin was almost translucent. I had to stare at them for a while before I could make out any features on their faces.

One was a middle-aged woman with luminous dark hair that framed an interesting and intelligent face. Her eyes were closed, and if it wasn't for the slight movement of her mouth, I would have thought she was gone. Then I looked over at the second prostrate angel and immediately stepped back. I couldn't believe my eyes.

"Henry," I whispered, barely able to get the word out. "Henry, is that you?" I rushed forward and grabbed his ice-cold hand. "It's me, it's me, Nicolas." My tears blinded me.

"You've got to be kidding," exclaimed Lucio.

CHAPTER 60

Wow," Serene said. "We awaken to such color."

We were again in the Realm, sitting under the tall, thick baobab tree from which we had started our journey to Earth. I marveled again at the tapestry of brightness that surrounded us after the dullness of Earth. Around the tree was a thick ring of wildflowers—purples, pinks, reds, and yellows surrounding us like a carpet of fallen rainbows.

Everything had happened quickly. We had just arrived at Leonardo's Woods when Magellan, Leonardo, and several others appeared and whisked Henry and the woman angel away. After they left, we three sat under the tree, gathering our thoughts and taking in the fact that we were home again.

I was worried about Henry. This was a new situation for the Realm. Angel stones had never been stolen like this, and Henry and the other angel were the first to be affected, so I knew the healers would be dealing with a new type of condition.

"He'll be okay," said Lucio suddenly, as if he knew what filled my thoughts. "I still can't believe the brilliance of the masters."

"What do you mean?" I asked.

"Well, Henry led you to your death, you haunted him to his, and now you've helped save him. Do you think this was all about reuniting you two?"

"Not all of it," said Serene grimly. "But whatever it was, brilliant or not, I'm just tired. I want to go back to the city, to my apartment and roommates," she complained.

Then I remembered. I hadn't yet told her or anyone else about Allie. For a moment, I considered telling them, but I was too exhausted to get into it at the moment. "I need to sleep," I said. "Do you think I'll be going back to Magellan's Chalet soon?"

"None of us can go home until we meet with the Council of Judgment tomorrow."

"What?"

"Oh, that's right. I forgot that you've never completed an assignment in a normal manner. Yes, we always have to meet with the Council the next day to go over everything."

"Yes, and with this one, they'll definitely want to go over how you two almost screwed everything up," snapped Serene, and she jumped up and walked away.

We all spent the night at Leonardo's, splayed out in front of his fireplace. He never returned while I was awake that evening, but at some point he must have, because I awoke to the smell of coffee. He was setting a table for us. A bowl of fresh biscuits and a pitcher of orange juice had already been laid out.

"Good morning!" he yelled loudly, waking the still-sleeping Lucio and Serene. "It is wonderful to see you young people back and having accomplished your assignment. You're off to the Council at eleven. I'll escort you, of course, but I will sit with the other members for the reckoning."

Reckoning. That didn't sound good.

I'd hoped that after a good night's sleep, the tension between Serene and Lucio would disappear, but I was wrong. At breakfast they ignored each other, and her anger seemed to extend to me. "What's it to you?" she barked, when I asked her if she was nervous about meeting with the Council.

"I was just curious," I retorted quietly.

"Well, it doesn't really matter, because if you ask me, it's going to be your and Lucio's asses on the line. You two messed up."

Her bluntness shocked me, and I reacted with silence. I was almost relieved when a carriage came about an hour later to escort us all to the Council Hall in the city. "I can't wait," I said aloud as we boarded. Lucio and Serene both rolled their eyes.

"Someone hasn't gone before the Council yet," said Lucio.

The Council Hall was quite foreboding, a somewhat crumbling gray medieval-style structure that looked like a castle. Once inside, we entered an empty, red-carpeted great room, its borders lined with wooden benches. As Lucio and I sat down on the nearest bench, Serene wandered away from us. I glanced up to the ceiling, which looked like an ever-expanding sky. At one end of the rectangular room was a narrow hallway that faced two tall golden doors.

"Don't you think this building is really cool?" Lucio asked.

"Sure," I said, not feeling the same way. I noticed that Serene had entered the narrow hallway.

"She's angry with me," Lucio said quietly.

"That's obvious," I responded. "What are you going to do about it?"

"I can't do anything. Falling in love with Julianne wasn't planned. It just happened. Serene needs to get over it."

"Do you think, as Serene does, that we'll be punished for our actions on this assignment?"

"Yes, yes I do," said Lucio solemnly. "Although we were successful, we messed up, Nic. Both of us."

"What will they do?"

"I don't know."

"You don't think I'll be sent away," I said, suddenly losing the confidence I had felt when I first regained the stones. "I can't bear it, just when I'm so close to being with Henry again."

"No, no, Nic," Lucio said, putting his hand on my shoulder. "I know it's not going to be that bad. They are fair, not vengeful, and you came through at the end, so calm down. They'll want to hear our account of the assignment. I suspect they'll call us in separately, but really, it won't be that bad."

I wasn't convinced.

"Other than Serene, we all pretty much broke the rules on this one," I said. "After all, I fell into Jared's hands through my own volition."

"Don't worry," Lucio reiterated. "I was the team leader and abandoned the team by falling in love with our assignment. I think I messed up more. Only Serene stayed on track."

Then we both heard a loud creak. The great golden double doors at the end of the hallway were opening. The Council's administrative clerk, a rather young-looking red-haired woman, stood there looking serious. "Lucio, we'd like to talk to you first."

I watched my friend make his way towards the Council and hoped for the best. It would be a long and trying day.

Hours passed, and Lucio didn't return. Serene, who eventually sat down next to me, drifted in and out of a sleep borne of boredom. At one point, a man appeared and gave us sandwiches and drinks. Then finally, after what seemed an eternity, the clerk came out again and called Serene in. About an hour later, it was my turn.

When I walked in, I was struck by how formal this proceeding would be. There were eight council members, including Leonardo, sitting along a long table in a room I had expected to be bigger. Dressed in black judges' robes, the council members were a mixed group of mostly older men and women. Everyone looked at me with serious eyes and taut mouths. All except

Leonardo. When I glanced at him, his eyes twinkled warmly, and it brought me some comfort. In front of the table was a lone chair backed in red velvet. The clerk waved me to it and I sat down.

"Nicolas Adams, will you tell us the truth about the events that occurred on Earth during your last assignment?" she asked.

"Ye—, yes," I stuttered nervously.

"Council, you may begin," the clerk stated.

The first to rise was a tall, thin man, who stared at me like a hungry bird that has spotted a worm. "I am Marchemay," he said. "And now I finally get to meet you, the boy who fell."

My mouth dropped. No one in the Realm had ever been so blunt about my status. "Yes, sir," I barely whispered.

"Did you know that we debated whether to give you a second chance in the Realm?" Marchemay said. "Did you know that, Nicolas? There were some of us who felt your spirit should remain trapped on Earth because you had chosen to stay so long in the darkness."

"Chosen?" I asked, feeling the accusation was unfair. "I didn't choose. I was trapped."

"No, boy. You weren't. You chose the darkness, just as you chose to confront and stay with Jared."

I looked down. Chosen? Had I really chosen that? I thought back to the horror of that time I had so wanted to forget. It took me a few minutes, but the truth of it came to me.

"Yes, you're right, Master Marchemay. I did choose the darkness, but it had to be. I had to be punished for haunting Henry."

It must have been the right thing to say, for I noticed that some at the table were nodding. But still Marchemay continued.

"We gave you another chance, and yet here you were, on your first assignment since, risking it all in anger and impatience. Encouraging Serene to commit a wrong and chasing

Jared, when your assignment was Julianne. What do you say to that?"

I could feel the heat rising in my cheeks and stayed mute.

The master turned to the panel. "There you have it. Silence from the boy, just as I imagined he would respond. We should suspend his status for good. He's not ready for the work." He sat back down at the table. It seemed as if my worst fears about being allowed to stay in the Realm might come true. My face blanched.

"Now, Marchemay, that is a little hasty, I feel. Give the boy a chance," Leonardo piped in.

"I don't think the Council should heed your interjection. You, after all, are his master, his mentor."

Then a discussion broke out among the others, until Leonardo stood up and began yelling above the din. "Tell them, Nicolas! Just tell them the truth about why you rebelled again."

"I feared," I said, "that I would not see my friend Henry again. It caused me to turn to Jared."

"Why did you fear it so much?" Leonardo asked. "Just tell us the truth. Come on, Nicolas, tell us."

Could I tell them the truth? Yes, yes, I would. There would be no more lies ever about how I felt about Henry.

"Because, because I love him," I said. "I love him as other men love women. There, there, I've said it aloud to you all. Henry is my soul mate, and I couldn't bear the thought that we would not be together again."

Slowly, a smile came to the master's face. "That's what we've been waiting to hear from you," Leonardo said. "You just need to be true to yourself. But getting back to your actions during this last assignment, even though your reasons are understandable, your actions themselves are not, so we will punish you, Nicolas."

Then the council members whispered among themselves for several minutes before Marchemay stood up again.

"Well, there must be some atonement," said Marchemay. "So for now we have decided that you will go back to Magellan's Chalet for more reflection and work, and you are temporarily suspended from your angel duties. If you progress, you will be upgraded again."

"Yes, sir," I said, wondering what lists of exhausting chores Magellan would set out for me.

I thought I was finished then, but the council members continued to question me, seeming especially interested in finding out about everything I had heard and experienced with Jared. It was then that I finally told them about Allie. The room burst out with loud voices of anger.

"Not another one!"

"What is happening in this place?"

"I can't believe it. Who would have thought that of her?"

The clerk yelled above the din, shouting, "Silence!" until everyone calmed down.

"We will deal with this situation separately," Marchemay said. "We are now done with you, Nicolas. Remember to continue to work hard so that you can regain your standing here in the Realm. You may leave now."

I walked out of the chamber. Jared was still loose on Earth with the power stones, Allie had not returned to the Realm, and other angels were still trapped. Yet even though that situation continued, to me it all seemed over with. I had done my part. Now I just wanted to be with Henry.

By the time I returned to Leonardo's, it was night, and Lucio and Serene were asleep on quilts near the fireplace in the front room. I joined them.

The next morning, the three of us sat slumped at the breakfast table, which only offered cold foods—fruit and cereal. The reckoning had tired us out, and we had all been ordered to head home today. We had been together for so long; I knew I would miss them, and I wanted to share my feelings. But the atmosphere was still tense. Serene and Lucio were silent and barely picked at their food. Perhaps this was for the best. Perhaps we all needed some time apart from each other.

"So it's goodbye then," I said to my teammates, standing up.

"Yes, goodbye," Serene repeated, getting up herself.

"Nicolas, wait," Lucio said. "And you too, Serene. I just wanted to say to both of you that your work on this assignment was exemplary. You both did what was needed, and ultimately we accomplished our goal. It was my honor to serve with you on this assignment."

"Thanks," I said. "I appreciate it."

Serene looked at Lucio, and then leaned over and hugged him before walking out the door. I had a feeling that in time they would be friends again.

CHAPTER 61

Two weeks passed, and still there was no news of Henry. I kept myself busy with chores and running errands for Magellan. In the afternoons, I meditated and reflected, as the masters had ordered. I knew I had to become a better angel, one with more faith in the order and will of the universe. One weekend, Lucio visited. Like me, he had been temporarily suspended from his angel duties, but the Council had already reinstated him. He was scheduled to go out on his first assignment the following week. He told me that he and Serene had still not made up; I told him I had faith it would happen.

Then, on the Wednesday after Lucio's visit, Magellan came out to me as I sat sketching and reading in the garden. Days earlier he had brought me a copy of *A Separate Peace* from one of the Realm's libraries, and I was now enjoying reading of the adventures of Gene and Phineas. I had started drawing my favorite scenes in my sketchbook.

"I have some news," Magellan said.

"Is it about Henry?"

"I don't know, but Leonardo wants you to go see him immediately."

"Now?"

"Yes, go," he said, smiling. I did not ask any questions, for I knew he had told me all he would. Instead I quickly packed for the long hike to Leonardo's hut and left Magellan's Chalet carrying the book, a basket of sandwiches, and water.

It took me a day to reach Leonardo's hut, and I hurried to knock on the front door just as Leonardo opened it. "Henry is waiting for you," he said.

"Where?" I said breathlessly.

"He's at the beach," he answered.

"A beach, in the Realm?"

"Yes, Nicolas, there is a beach here too," he said, noticing my surprised expression. "Just follow the straight path through the woods, and it will lead you to some fields, then the sand dunes where he's waiting."

"Thank you," I said hurriedly and continued my journey. I ran through Leonardo's Woods and out through sunflower-filled fields, and finally, as a full moon rose over a darkened sky, I reached a series of high sand dunes. After some exhausting uphill walking, I could finally see the shoreline. And there, there in the light of a full moon, was Henry. My breath caught in my throat, and I had to stop walking for a moment, for I feared I would fall. I noticed my hands were shaking.

Henry stood in the white moonlight, staring out at the purple-tinged sea. Waves crashed in front of him, sweeping over his bare feet. The wind blew his dark hair from his features, reminding me of our time on the *Mary Selina*, when on some of the bright, beautiful days, we would stand on deck and stare out at the endless horizon. Henry, in a checkered shirt and rolled-up beige slacks, looked radiant in the brilliant moonlight of the Realm. He had definitely recovered.

He suddenly turned around and looked up at me as I ran down the sandy expanse that led to the shore. I stopped in front of him, and we both stood stiff, as if frozen—in shock that we were finally together after so many years.

"You are a sight," he said.

Then suddenly a broad smile broke over his face. "I prayed it would be you," he said. "The masters just told me there was someone I was to meet with out here."

"Finally," I said. "It's only been nearly two hundred years."

We laughed.

There was much to say, but we were overwhelmed and instead sat silently by the shore for a few minutes. It was Henry who spoke first, broaching an easier subject than the circumstances of the last time we'd seen each other.

"Have you reunited with your mother and father?" he asked.

"No. Not yet. I have no idea where they are. Eventually I know it will happen. But all this time, I focused my thoughts on finding you. I had to find you."

He looked over at me but said nothing.

"What about you? Where's your family?" I asked.

"Father and Mother came to see me while I was recovering. They're both at a higher dominion, and my sisters have all been reborn to Earth for several cycles now. And guess who is a friend of mine here in the Realm?"

"Who?"

"Shelley. She is an assistant to a master and is doing well."

"That's great."

"You know, Nic, I've been sailing here in the Realm. We can go sailing. Would you like that?"

"That would be great," I said, thrilled at the prospect of enjoying a sail, just the two of us. But then we were silent again. I knew there was so much more we needed to discuss beyond this small talk. It was Henry who spoke first again.

"Just where have you been all this time, Nic?" he asked. "When I killed myself, I had so hoped to see you."

"I've been to a place you never want to go to, Henry. I fell."

"I'm sorry," he said. "It's my fault. Words don't seem enough to express the amends I must make to you."

"No, stop," I said. "It is I who need forgiveness. Please tell me you've forgiven me for haunting you, for judging you, for everything. I was so angry at you, and when I learned you were engaged, I became even angrier. I thought you had forgotten me and had stopped loving me."

Tears appeared in his dark eyes.

"I could never forget you, nor stop loving you. But I too am so sorry, Nic. Can you ever, ever forgive me for letting you take the punishment for what I did?"

"I have," I answered. "I finally have."

He closed his eyes and released a sigh of relief.

"I have wanted to hear that for so long," he said. "You know, I wanted to do the right thing after you were murdered. I tried to make amends during my life. While on the ship, I put myself in danger many times so that others would be safe, but it was all for naught, for I knew I had failed you and that there was no way I could make up for my misdeed against you by helping someone else. So when you haunted me, I thought the only real way to make amends was by sacrificing my own life. After my death, I learned that was an error too, because I caused suffering to my family, friends, and fiancée. I promise now, in whatever way I can, I will be a good friend to you, Nic."

"Yes, I know," I said.

We stared at each other for a minute. "So we're friends again," he said, reaching out his hand to shake mine.

"More than that," I said, throwing my arms around his shoulders and hugging him tightly. We held each other for a long time, and it felt wonderful to feel his body against mine. Then we looked at each other, and Henry leaned in; our lips met, met finally, after so long, and it was right to kiss him that way.

THE END

ACKNOWLEDGMENTS

A special thanks to the talented and supportive staff at Girl Friday Productions; the novel's first editor, Neil Plakcy; and writing group members Diana Levy, Paul Rottenberg, and Art Saluk, who commented on the early drafts of this work. I am also in gratitude to my husband, Richard, whose own out-at-sea experiences were always a ready resource. Finally, I'd like to acknowledge and thank all the great sea-story tellers whose works inspired me to want to write my own ocean tale, especially Herman Melville, Nathaniel Philbrick, C.S. Forester, and Laurence Bergreen.

ABOUT THE AUTHOR

A former journalist, Lourdes R. Florido has been published in the *Sun Sentinel*, *South Florida Parenting Magazine*, and other publications. She now teaches English as a professor at Broward College in Florida. She received a First Place Award of Merit from the Writers' Network of South Florida for her nonfiction piece "The Cuban Me," and her young adult novel, *White Trees*, received an honorable mention in the Independent Publisher Book Awards. *A Whisper of Angels* is the first book in the Nuevos Angels series. Lourdes, who was born in Havana, Cuba, now resides in South Florida with her husband and dogs.